The Crime of a Christmas Toy

Henry Herman

First published: London, 1893

This edition published 2022 by

OREON

an imprint of

The Oleander Press
16 Orchard Street
Cambridge
CB1 1JT

www.oleanderpress.com

A CIP catalogue record for the book
is available from the British Library.

ISBN: 9781915475169

Cover design, typesetting & ebook: neorelix

Contents

For first news of titles, give-aways and discounts, sign up to our infrequent newsletter at: oleanderpress.com

Chapter 1

The Shadow of Death

Lord Senfrey glanced over the letter which his valet had handed to him, and his face darkened. He pursed his lips and gently patted Sprat, the little Yorkshire terrier that lay snugly curled up on his lap. Then, having mechanically read the epistle twice, or perhaps thrice, he looked up from it and around the room after the manner of a man so annoyed that he does not know whither his train of thoughts is leading him. The valet was standing on the other side of the table, whereon his lordship's untouched breakfast lay. Like the good and polished servant he was, he appeared to be deeply interested in the progress of two or three flies that were perambulating upon the ceiling. He knew that his lordship was unusually vexed from the impatient tapping of his lordship's forefinger upon the tablecloth.

Lord Senfrey leant back in his armchair and, crossing his hands in front of him, so that the thumbs stood upwards, stared at the missive lying on the table, while the little old doggie, in seeming wonderment at the sudden motion which disturbed his comfort, sat upon his haunches and looked into his master's face in plaintive remonstrance.

"What a nuisance that man is!" his lordship said at last. "You told him that I was not at home?"

"Yes, my lord," replied the valet; "but he answered that he knew your lordship was at home, and that he would wait, if he had to do it, all day to see you."

Another pause – during which the continued tapping of the forefinger was the only sound audible in the room.

"I had better see him, I suppose," said Lord Senfrey, whilst his eyes wandered hither and thither, as if to escape that horrid letter on the table. "I vow I'll never do a service to such creatures again. It isn't my fault that she has disappeared. All I did was to help her to an engagement."

He waited for a moment, as if expecting a word of approval from his servant.

"You know it, Morton," he went on bitterly, "you know all about the business. You, of all people, know very well that I had nothing to do with the girl's disappearance. I wish to Heaven that I had never had anything to do with her at all."

The astute Morton, still keeping his eyes upon the ceiling, as if endeavouring to find there a solution of the enigma which bothered his lordship, said, in the quietest possible tone of voice:

"If you were to ask my opinion, my lord – which, of course, I wouldn't venture to offer for the world without being asked – I would—"

The valet paused, as if afraid of having overstepped the barriers of duty and service.

"What would you say, Morton? – out with it," questioned Lord Senfrey.

"I would say," the valet rejoined, "that it was a case of blackmail."

Lord Senfrey sat upright. Sprat, for a second time in a short space shaken from his place, jumped on the table by the side of his lordship's plate, and looked with envious eyes upon the silver cover, from beneath which the odour of grilled chop reached his nostrils. His lordship noticed the old doggie's reproof, and, with a tender hand, replaced him upon his lap.

"You're a clever fellow, Morton," he exclaimed. "You know the world a lot better than I do, and I often think that I know it a great deal too well. You've hit it. It's a case of blackmail. Now you've suggested the idea, I'm sure it's a case of blackmail. The girl has disappeared, nobody seems to know whither, nobody seems to know why, nor with whom. For all I know, that blackguard Italian may have conspired with his sister, and he comes to me as if I were hiding her.

"It's a confounded nuisance," he went on, "but I shall have to settle it one way or the other. I won't be bothered like that for nothing, just now of all the times in the year. I won't drag such a millstone from my bachelor state into my married life. I've got quite enough to answer for of my own doing without being worried by people who have no claims whatever upon me. Let the man come up."

Morton bowed and left.

Lord Senfrey, who was thus disturbed on the very morning before the day appointed for his marriage with Lady Georgina Rhowdon, only daughter and heiress of the Earl of Bent, was a decidedly popular man. Most people in this world thought him one of the luckiest men in it.

He was not born to the title. When he was a lad some five or six lives stood between him and the barony, its myriads of acres, and its mighty rent-roll. His father had been but a country clergyman, with a stipend of five hundred a year, and a family of six children to keep. Young Alfred Neymer was sent to an army tutor, and with the help of the former Lord Senfrey and of other relatives, a commission was purchased for him.

But his career in the army was short, though his bravery was conspicuous, and acknowledged by his superiors on more than one glorious occasion. He was a bad soldier, as far as obedience and discipline were concerned. On one occasion he saved an important line of communication by flagrant disobedience of orders, coupled with a desperate valour, which reduced his command to one half of its numbers.

The Horse Guards grumblingly acknowledged the achievement, but in less than four months – on the occasion of a less brilliant breach of discipline – Captain Neymer was compelled to resign. After that he led a rough life of adventure in the Australian bush and in the wilds of America – an existence extremely chequered, and not always inclining towards prosperity.

In the meantime one life after the other that stood between him and the peerage was swept away, until one morning Alfred Neymer, then at his wit's ends how to live, received a letter styling him "My Lord."

It was but natural that a nobleman who burst upon London Society with such a thrilling record, and who, with great wealth, combined with an attractive exterior, should become one of the lions of the day. Lord Senfrey was a handsome man, tall, straight-limbed, and broad-chested, looking every inch a soldier.

He was rich. The Senfrey estates were vast and totally unencumbered. He was popular in the clubs and popular in the drawing rooms. All the men called him "good fellow," and the ladies thought him delightful. The whiffs of scandal which now and then floated across Mayfair salons concerning him never went far enough to seriously tarnish his reputation.

Belgravian mothers-in-law admitted that it was better that Lord Senfrey should sow his wild oats before marriage than to bring a stock of the undesirable commodity to a newly-wedded wife. The young ladies, when they heard the subject mentioned, vowed it too awfully wicked, but admired the fortunate nobleman all the more. There was not one of them who would not have gladly undertaken the task of guiding the straying sheep to the folds of holy wedlock.

With all that, Lord Senfrey was neither better nor worse than the average man who, after a long life of exposure and trial, suddenly finds himself the possessor of great wealth. He had not been a month in town before various rumours were afloat concerning an intimacy between him and Dorothy Anderson, a handsome young actress, whose portraits at that period graced most of the photographers' shop windows. Other reports were abroad, one especially about his interest in an Italian girl, Maria Orano, the sister of a young sculptor of rising reputation.

Somehow or other these rumours died away. His lordship had evidently learned discretion with experience, and though he was a *habitué* of the stage-side of certain theatres, no really serious allegation could thenceforth be brought against him. Thus it came on the very next day after this commencement of our history he was to be married to the only daughter of the great Earl of Bent.

And yet, as we have seen, Lord Senfrey had reason to be annoyed.

He took the silver cover from the plate, and cutting a small piece for himself and another for Sprat, left his own morsel untouched, while the dog quickly finished his portion. A sip or two of coffee and a tiny piece of toast were all that passed his lips before the valet returned, followed by a tall, slim, dark-haired man – the very type of the southern Italian.

The man was dressed after the fashion of the better class of artists, in a black velvet coat and waistcoat, with the ends of his black silk neckerchief dangling loosely in front of him. His rather good-looking face was blanched – of that creamy pallor which only extreme emotion can produce on a dark skin. He stood still on the threshold and looked at Lord Senfrey as if he could have jumped at him and torn him to pieces. His hands were behind his back, and he bit his lips silently.

Lord Senfrey turned round to the man and said gruffly, "Now, sir, your business. What do you want with me?"

The man's reply was savage. His enunciation was slow, and his Italian accent emphasized it.

"Reparation reparation," he said slowly.

Lord Senfrey felt that his wrath was getting the better of him, and gripped his right hand with his left to compose himself.

"Reparation!" he exclaimed fiercely. "For what?"

"For my sister."

Lord Senfrey rose and looked the man straight in the face.

"I'm tired of this," he said quietly, "I'm tired of you and your sister both. You know as well as I do that all I ever did were two or three acts of kindness to her. You know as well as I do that I was no more to her than my servant there. I know nothing about her disappearance and don't want to know, and if you come here bothering me again I will call the police and have you taken into custody."

The man stood unmoved.

"Call in police," he said. "I am ready."

He stepped to the chair next to him and sat himself down.

The valet, thinking it was time to test the effect of his advice upon his lordship, asked: "Shall I go for a constable?"

Lord Senfrey shrugged his shoulders with a sickly smile. "What for, Morton?" he asked.

"To take this man away."

A smile spread again upon Lord Senfrey's features.

"When I want to throw that man into the street, Morton," he said, "I shall require no aid, and he won't fall softly when I handle him."

The man's sullen determination had roused the stalwart soldier to his former self-reliance. He pulled out his watch and laid it upon the table.

"I'm going to give you one minute," he said, "to tell me exactly what you want from me. At the end of that minute, I'm going to take you by the scruff of the neck and throw you into the street; and if you dare to ring my bell again, I shall instruct my servants to give you into custody. Now, what do you want?"

"Reparation," was the slow and long-drawn reply again; "reparation for my sister's death."

It was now Lord Senfrey's turn to feel the colour fading from his cheeks.

"Your sister's death?" he asked hoarsely. "Your sister is dead?"

"Yes," replied the man, "my sister dead."

"But how? – and where?" asked Lord Senfrey.

"She was found this morning in little room where she live a week past. She poison herself."

"I am very sorry," said Lord Senfrey, "very sorry indeed to hear this. But what have I to do with it? I know nothing whatever about her. I give you my word of honour, I am as innocent of any connection with her death as you are yourself."

The man rose.

"Your word of honour!" he sneered. "My name Luigi Orano. Te Orano were princes tousand year ago. You an English nobleman. My sister happy till she know you. You say you not know her. My sister dead. You lie!"

Lord Senfrey, without further ado, crossed to the man and gripped him by the throat. The door was standing open, and though the Italian kicked and fought and bit, the iron fingers inserted themselves between his neck and his neckcloth and, twisting the latter, half strangled him. Thus he was dragged and bumped, step by step, down the stairs, along the hall – where the astonished footman, guessing his master's intention, opened the door – and flung like a bundle of rags into the street.

"See to it, Bradley," said his lordship to the footman. "If that man rings my bell again, give him into custody."

Signor Orano, however, seemed to have no desire, for that moment at any rate, to revisit Lord Senfrey's inhospitable roof. He rose scowlingly and gnashed his teeth and shook his fist.

"Birbante!" he exclaimed, brushing the dust from his clothing and rearranging his disordered neckcloth. "Beware! Beware! I come again!"

With that he pulled himself together and, breathing heavily, limped slowly away.

The day had evidently dawned ominously for the house of Neymer, for whilst its noble chief was worried and vexed by what he considered an attempt at blackmail, his younger brother received a visitor, even less welcome than Signor Orano, at Eaton Square.

Martin Neymer was Lord Senfrey's younger brother, and next in line of succession to the title and estates. He resembled his brother in nothing but his height. He was tall, but had none of Lord Senfrey's athletic build, none of his frankness of countenance, none of his handsome, soldier-like appearance.

Although two years younger than his lordship, he looked fully twenty years his senior. His face was always smoothly shaven and very pale. The forehead was already wrinkled, and beneath the deep-sunken, restless eyes, crows' feet crossed on to the cheeks. His hair was sparse and nearly white. He looked essentially the man he was – weak, undecided, and easily swayed for good or for evil.

Martin Neymer's visitor was no less a personage than Mr. Muir Macrae, the well-known Duke Street money-lender and bill discounter, an oily gentleman, upon whose thick lips and square jaw pearled the most benign of smiles. Mr. Macrae's broad face was fringed by a sandy beard of huge proportions, whilst the long upper lip was undefiled by any hirsute appendage. He was a portly gentleman, black frock-coated, and black silk waist-coated, and wore an old-fashioned stock, whilst from his fob dangled some half dozen massive seals.

Mr. Macrae was standing with his hands behind his back, looking over his gold spectacles at Mr. Martin Neymer, who sat in his armchair by his table, even paler than usual. Mr. Martin Neymer's lips were ashen, and he looked about him like one dazed.

"Confess et," Mr. Macrae was saying, "confess et, sir, that segnature of Lorrd Senfrey is a forgery."

"How dare you!" Martin Neymer replied haggardly. "How dare you suggest such a thing, sir!"

"Ah dare do what is reet. The bank don't lie, and the bank says that's nae Lorrd Senfrey's segnature."

"It's a mistake," explained Neymer. "It's quite a mistake, Mr. Macrae, I assure you. You shall be paid your two thousand pounds. If you'll let me have the bill, I'll get you the money for it."

"Quite so," retorted Mr. Macrae. "Ah've nae doubt ye'll mak et reet. But ye maun delay. Ah want my money – nae mair, nae less."

"You shall have your money," said Neymer nervously. This whole miserable business is a mistake which I cannot explain. I'll go and see my brother today, and you shall have the two thousand pounds in less than a week."

"Nae," was the dry rejoinder, "not a week. Ah'll gie ye tell tomorrow – tomorrow at noon. At one o'clock ah wash my hands, and ah'll put the business into my lawyer's keeping. Now ye know what ah want, Mr. Neymer, and let me tell ye that ye ought to be thankful that ah'm dealing sae friendly wi ye. Guid-morning."

The portly Scot took his hat from the chair on which he had placed it, and turning upon his heel, walked out without another word.

Martin Neymer sat at his table for some moments as if the world were dead to him, and his surroundings existed not. He did not even hear the movement of a door at the further end of the room, nor did he see his wife who stood there.

Mrs. Neymer was nearly as tall as her husband, with a face that had been handsome, with a kind of cruel, classic beauty, and eyes that still flashed like black gems. She was dressed in a loose morning wrapper of the finest and softest Liberty silk, bordered by a foam of precious lace.

She stood on the threshold and looked at her husband, shaking her head as if in mute reproach. She approached the table without being heard, and paused at her husband's side for a score of seconds, without a word. At last she tapped him on the shoulder, and he looked up. His eyes met hers, and he shrank back shuddering.

"Well!" she exclaimed stoically.

"It is all over, Agatha," he mourned. "I'm found out. That man, Macrae, has discovered that Alfred's signature was forged."

"Well!" the lady repeated, without a trace of emotion. "Surely you expected that he would discover that? Surely you were prepared for that discovery?"

"What do you mean, Agatha?" asked the husband, in a hoarse tremor.

"I mean," the wife answered, in a voice of perfect commonplace, "that, as a matter of course, you've been to your brother and got from him the two thousand pounds to pay the bill."

Neymer looked into his wife's eyes with a face so pitiful that it might have moved a stone, but the lady merely laughed.

"What a wry face you're making, Martin," she said. "I've no patience with you. I can see by your looks that you've done absolutely nothing – that you have allowed this to come upon you, as you knew it would, and that you've not the means to square it."

"I haven't a fifty-pound note, and that man wants two thousand pounds," groaned the man.

"Well," remonstrated Mrs. Neymer quietly, "go to Alfred and get the money."

"I can't," replied the husband. "He gave me a thousand pounds only three weeks ago, and you've had it nearly all, Agatha – nearly every penny of it."

"I was bound to pay my bills," the lady replied. "If I didn't pay my bills I should have nothing to wear. Mrs. Simmonds wanted seven hundred pounds, and I gave her four hundred. I owed three hundred and sixty pounds to Hughes, the bookmaker, and that had to be paid, of course. And then I bought a pony to match Nero. I paid nearly a hundred pounds for him. So you see I hadn't much left."

The worried husband looked at his wife for a few heartbeats' space meekly.

"I don't reproach you, Agatha," he said. "You know that if I had it, I'd give you all you could wish for, and more. But you are extravagant, Agatha. Your style of living has brought us to this. We must retrench, Agatha; we must. I can't continually go to Alfred and ask him for money. It's not right, and he'll get tired of it, especially now when he is going to get married and will have a wife to keep—"

"A wife," sneered the lady, "A wife who has ten thousand a year in her own right. I wish I had ten thousand a year."

"If you had ten thousand a year, my dear," rejoined Neymer, "you would spend ten thousand more. But that would make no difference. You should have it if I could give it you; but I can't. I've come to the end of my tether, and I suppose it's only right that this should fall upon me. The man who does a criminal act ought to suffer for it, and I've committed a criminal act."

"Don't talk nonsense," exclaimed the lady. "It isn't your fault that, by the stupid laws of this country, your brother is worth millions and you are penniless. If that brother of yours were out of the way, I would be Lady Senfrey, and I would be able to live as I ought to live."

The eyes flashed more bitterly than before, and the bosom heaved as if in resentment, whilst for a second, and a second only, a hot flush came to the lady's cheeks, and her face became clouded as if a dark thought were crossing her mind.

"Don't lose any time," she burst out at last, "go to your brother. He'll have to give you that two thousand pounds, and he will give it to you. Now I must run away and dress, else I shall be late for the private view."

She shrugged her shoulders contemptuously, and walked to the other end of the room.

"If I were only Lady Senfrey," she said to herself. Then she paused, and her eyes flashed back to her husband. "Who knows!" she hissed under her breath, and went to her own room.

Lord Senfrey was still sitting over his unfinished breakfast when his brother was announced. He was well accustomed to these matutinal visits; and when he saw Martin pale as a sheet, and with eyes even more shifty than usual, he immediately recognised that his brother was in trouble for money.

It had been a source of grim, humorous satisfaction to him to help his brother in season and out of season. He was a bachelor, and his wants were few. He did not spend one tithe of his income, and would not have known how to do it satisfactorily to himself if he had tried. He had lent his brother thousands where he had spent hundreds upon himself, but gradually he had come to appreciate that the more he lent the more his brother's wife wanted; and though he was perfectly prepared to enable Martin Neymer to live in a style befitting the brother of a peer, he rebelled at being called upon to satisfy Mrs. Martin Neymer's wanton and foolish extravagance.

"What's up now, Martin?" he asked, rather peevishly. "Has that wife of yours run through all that money already?"

"I'm in awful trouble, Alfred," replied the younger brother, seating himself by Lord Senfrey's side, "and I want you to help me out of it just this once."

"Oh, I know what it is," answered Lord Senfrey. "It's 'only this time' until the next."

"I promise you I'll insist upon retrenchment if you'll help me over this," rejoined Martin, in hoarse gutturals.

Lord Senfrey rose and went to his desk. There he took his cheque-book and returned to the table.

"You've had a great deal of money from me lately, Martin; but I don't mind. I don't want to be bothered with a recital of your woes. I'm out of temper already, and I don't want to be out of temper when I meet Georgina this morning."

He wrote out a cheque for five hundred pounds.

"Here," he said, "take this. This ought to help you over the next month, at any rate."

Martin took the piece of paper and glanced at it with burning eyes.

"I was going to ask you—" he said.

"I do – not – want to be bothered, Martin," said Lord Senfrey firmly. "Take this, and leave me in peace on the day before my marriage."

"But this won't help me, Alfred," feebly remonstrated the trembling Martin.

Again he was interrupted.

"Surely five hundred pounds will keep you from starvation for a while! Come to me again in a fortnight, if you like, but leave me alone now."

"I must have two thousand pounds, Alfred," pleaded Martin.

Lord Senfrey rose and looked his brother straight in the face. "Look here, Martin," he said; "you are my brother, and I'll do anything in the world to serve you, but I'm not going to continue to let your wife fling my money out of the window. You have five hundred pounds there. As I said before, this will help you for a while, "and it must help you. Now, do please leave me."

There was nothing left for the poor man but to take what was given him and to go.

"Thank you, Alfred," he said. "I quite appreciate what you say, and, of course, you are quite right – absolutely right – only—"

"Do have some commiseration for a man," interrupted Lord Senfrey. "I've told you that in a fortnight you can come to me again, but I want to be left in peace this morning. I've said it, and mean it."

"Thank you, Alfred," said Martin quietly, and walked out in stony despair.

While Lord Senfrey was writing out his cheque, Sprat had been busy with his lordship's breakfast. He was a pampered little doggie, and had shared his master's poverty as he was now sharing his wealth. Lord Senfrey smiled at his little four-footed friend, and patted his head.

"It doesn't cost much to keep you, Sprat," he said, "and you're the only true and faithful creature about me in this world, after all – just now, at any rate."

The little old doggie wriggled and wagged his tail in seeming acknowledgment of his master's eulogy. Then he pressed his cold muzzle against his master's cheek, and Lord Senfrey's face brightened.

"What's the good of annoying one's self?" he muttered. "What do I care, after all? I know that, whatever that man may say, I am absolutely innocent. It hasn't been so in everything, but in this case Heaven knows my hands are clean. I suppose there'll be a coroner's inquest, and a scandal. Well," – he heaved a great sigh, "it will be an occasion to try Georgina's love for me, and her faith in me."

Dressing, with Lord Senfrey, always occupied a short space of time, but as the morning wore on, his spirits brightened. A gallop along the Row quickened his circulation, and when he met his bride he was in the best possible humour. The day passed pleasantly indeed. There were a hundred and one things to do which fall to every man's lot on his bridal eve, and with the petty excitement resulting from his occupation the trouble of the morning was forgotten.

In the evening Lord Senfrey gave his last bachelor party, and a dozen friends – tried chums most of them – sat down to dinner.

That, too, was over and the faithful Morton was waiting in his lordship's own room with a small parcel of letters and other missives. As was his habit, he assisted Lord Senfrey to his dressing gown and slippers, and, having put everything ready for the night, awaited further orders.

"I don't think I shall look through these letters tonight, Morton," said Lord Senfrey, when a small parcel attracted his gaze. It was a packet about five or six inches long, three inches broad, and about an inch deep, and was neatly addressed in imitation of printed characters. It was marked "personal and immediate."

Sprat had jumped on the table, and made little darts at the box, as if he were endeavouring to drag it out of Lord Senfrey's hands. He snarled and sat up and begged effusively, and then snarled again.

"Quiet, be quiet, Sprat," said Senfrey, caressing the doggie. "This is for me, and not for you."

Sprat growled all the more, sat up, and begged again. The little paws went up and down in a swift quiver, and he made another dart at the box, and sneezed, and shook his little head and sneezed again. Lord Senfrey patted his old canine friend, and placed him on the armchair by his side.

"You must be quiet, Sprat," he said; "I want to have a look at this. It's a present, I suppose, from somebody who wishes to disguise his identity," he added.

So saying, he tore off the paper which wrapped it, and found a second covering of plain white paper, and on it were written, in handwriting similar to the address, the words, "From a friend; a present for tomorrow."

"I told you I knew what it was, Morton," said his lordship gaily.

He removed that covering too, and found a tin box, such as is often used for packing Egyptian or Turkish cigarettes. He tore it open with a quick movement, and immediately there resounded through the room a sharp report, like that which is heard when young people at Christmas pull explosive crackers.

At the same time something fumed and hissed and seethed in the open box, and a column of thick brownish smoke curled swiftly upwards and struck Lord Senfrey full in the face and enveloped him. The poor man gasped like a fish that is flung out of the water on to the grass, and fell forward, right into the horrible vapour.

The diabolic substance in the box fumed and crackled all the more. The brown smoke became thicker and more voluminous, and Sprat, who had jumped on the table, made a dart towards his master, but flew away again, howling piteously.

Morton rushed towards Lord Senfrey for the purpose of dragging him away; but the fiendish smoke struck him. He had to fly for dear life towards one of the windows, which he flung open wide, and, gasping, held on to the sill, while the venomous smoke crept around the room and filled it. Sprat whined as a child might have cried.

Morton, creeping along the wall with his handkerchief before his nose and mouth, managed to reach the second window, to push it open, and, half strangled, staggered on to the balcony, where Sprat followed him, howling. When his eyes burned a little less, and he recovered his power of speech, Morton cried for help, and passers-by, attracted by his shouts, roused the servants below, who came rushing upstairs helter-skelter and threw open the door.

But the room was one mass of rolling, poisonous haze; and though a current of fresh air was established, entrance was impossible. Strong men, desperately endeavouring to reach their master, whom they could see lying in the Satanic mist, with his head on the table, had to retire in ghastly horror.

A good many minutes passed before either Morton or the other servants could reach Lord Senfrey, and when they carried the limp and prostrate figure to the bed, and laid it there, they found that life was extinct.

Sprat had crept on to his dead master's bed, and, whining as if his little heart were breaking, licked the cold, white face.

Chapter 2

A Greyhound in the Slips

The London season was at its height when society was startled and all the world was shocked by the simultaneous announcements of Maria Orano's suicide and of Lord Senfrey's murder. Society, consisting, of course, of nice people only, immediately laid the foul murder to the charge of the plebeian foreigner who had threatened Lord Senfrey. The world at large, being actuated by more communistic ideas, came to a similar conclusion; but added a rider to its verdict – namely, that if Lord Senfrey had driven the girl to the poisoned cup, he had only got his deserts if the brother had avenged his sister's death.

The world at large, being rather purblind, considered the "if" as of little virtue, and from saying "if" timidly and without vigour, came gradually to omitting it altogether. Luigi Orano was immediately arrested on suspicion, and remanded, pending enquiries.

The two inquests were summoned for the same day; that upon Lord Senfrey at the Eaton Square mansion, that upon poor Maria Orano in the Holborn Town Hall in Gray's Inn

Road, as she had poisoned herself in a lodging in James Street, Bedford Row.

The doctors were at loggerheads about the exact means by which Lord Senfrey had met his death, but they all agreed that he died from paralysis of the heart, the contractions of the vital organ having been stopped by perfect paralysis of the cardiac ganglia of the sympathetic nerve. They were also agreed that death most likely occurred suddenly and swiftly. The only further indication which they obtained to guide their opinion was the extreme contraction of the iris.

Having got so far as to acknowledge that Lord Senfrey was undoubtedly killed by the inhalation of a cerebrocardiac poison, they agreed to disagree upon the actual venom used for the purpose; and, in fact, having very little indication to guide them, none of them ventured to express a decided opinion.

My full patronymic is George Patrick Edward Victor Sandon Molyneux Grey, but I call myself George Grey, and my friends call me "G. G.," because, they say, I am as strong as a horse, and can go as fast.

My dear, dead dad, Major-General Sir Patrick Grey, was wounded at the Alma, and had to retire. Besides his pension, he had at that time an income of fully two thousand a year from his Irish estates. Before he died, the good old gentleman saw that rent-roll dwindle down to one thousand, then to six hundred, and then to five hundred; and when he was laid to his last rest, it was three hundred all told.

I was, at that time, walking the hospitals, and poor dad had been struggling his hardest to keep me and my two delicate sisters in a style fitting our station. With his death, of course, his pension ceased. The estates and their appurtenant income reverted to me; but I thought that a great hulking fellow like myself had much less right to the three hundred a year than my sisters, so I have since then handed over to them my Irish agent's cheques.

Of course, I had to earn my own living and to leave the hospitals. As good luck favoured me, I managed to obtain a secretaryship to a wealthy Radical M.P.; and through him I acquired such a knowledge of London, its tricks and its trickeries, its crimes and its criminals, as I could never have otherwise obtained outside of a police office.

All kinds of investigations were entrusted to me, and I can even now revert to them with pride. My Radical M.P. got thrown out at the General Election, and went abroad in a huff. I then determined to make use of the knowledge I had acquired to start in business as a private detective.

When the Senfrey murder became the all-engrossing subject of conversation, I had established myself prosperously in my little office and chambers in Craven Street, Strand. I was engaged at the time in an enquiry relating to the doings, or misdoings, of Count Gyffa Brodie, a Levantine nobleman who had crossed the sacred portals of London Society by means of excellent introductions, and who, during his short stay among London Society people, had managed to meet with extraordinary luck at cards. He was a member, honorary or regular, of two or three clubs much frequented by the *jeunesse dorée*. His recommendations had been unimpeachable.

His manner was distinguished, his appearance and style of dress elegant. Among the committeemen of the Olympian Club, however, there were two or three bluff, hard-headed old soldiers who did not at all relish Count Gyffa Brodie's triumphal career – as far as their club was concerned, at any rate. One of these, General Massinger, a war and weather-bronzed old Indian, came to me and asked me to take the matter in hand.

"Not that I can say a word about the fellow, George," he said; "but I don't like him."

"My dear General," I argued, "that's no indication of dishonesty or even of ungentlemanly conduct on the man's part."

"Hang me," said the General, "if I had any proof I'd soon fling him out. I want you to get me proof."

"But," I went on, "supposing the man is what he says he is, and we have no right to suppose anything else, how am I to get proof?"

"Oh!" said the General, in his stubborn old disciplinarian fashion, "I don't like the man, and when I don't like a man I know he's a rogue. You'll prove he's a rogue all right. Go on; I'll pay the piper."

I went on, and shortly before the time when the Senfrey murder came like a thunderbolt out of a clear sky upon London, I had come to the conclusion that the old soldier was perhaps right in his surmises about Count Gyffa Brodie.

When I read the accounts of the Senfrey affair in the papers, I said to myself, "That's the sort of pie in which I should like to have a finger." It was bound to be a tough case, and a tough case was just what I wanted. The more mysterious and the more unfathomable, the better I would have liked it.

The old adage says that "poets are born; they cannot be made." I verily believe the saying applies to detectives. It seemed to me as if I had been born to the business, and the detective instinct was strong in me. I panted to get a chance to unravel this mystery, and the opportunity, as it happened, was afforded me.

My father had always been on terms of intimacy with the Earl of Bent. I remember well, in my Eton-jacket days, playing on the lawn of Farlowe Towers, down Yorkshire way, with Lady Georgina Rhowdon, the earl's only daughter, then a pretty girl of five or six. She was a delicate little lady at the time, and impressed me as being too frail to be made of flesh and blood – her hands were so tiny, her skin so transparent, and her eyes, even at that early age, so limpid and languid.

The earl was a widower at that time, and was a great chum of my father's. The two old gentlemen both frequented the same club, and were of the same politics to a shade, held the same views on Church matters, and were interested in the same hobbies, with the only difference that my old dad was comparatively poor, and Lord Bent was very rich.

From my boyish days forward I had looked upon Lord Bent with a peculiar kind of awe. I had heard my father speak about him as a man who was able to do what he, my father, could not, and this impressed my young mind with a sense of the peculiar importance to the State, to society, and to the world at large, of the great master of Farlowe Towers. Yet he was a little man – barely five feet four, perhaps – as thin as a rat condemned to roam about a church, and perhaps as lithe in his movements.

He had a pleasant face, though a sharp one; always smooth-shaven, except for small white whiskers. His glossy white hair was always smoothly parted and nicely brushed, and he was about as affable, as unpretentious, and as nice an old gentleman as you might meet anywhere.

When he strolled along the walk in Hyde Park, with his hands behind his back and his stick dangling from his fingers, bowing pleasantly right and left, and smiling all the while, one might have taken him for an old professor recognising and being recognised by a large number of grateful pupils.

Georgina, at the time of the commencement of this our history, had grown into a beauty of the fragile and exotic kind. She resembled her father in the smallness of her build, though she was a trifle taller. Her skin was of the palest, and most translucent. Her hair, which was of that delicate brown that glitters with a sheen of gold or bronze, according to the light that falls upon it, set off and rendered more delicate the creamy pallor of her complexion.

Her eyes attracted everybody's gaze – large, round, dark blue, and dreamy. There was a languor about her movements and a mellow softness about her manner which made people wonder that she had accepted as her future husband so bluff, hardy, and stalwart a soldier as Lord Senfrey. The old earl doted upon her. She was his only child, and in her he thought he saw a delicate and idealised image of his dear dead wife.

If there was anybody to dispute Lady Georgina Rhowdon's place in her father's heart, that person was the present Lady Bent – Lord Bent's second wife – a tall, stately lady who had passed the line which divides woman's existence on this earth, and had stepped well into the forties. The hand of time drops lightly upon some women, however, and Lady Bent, when looking her best, and when dressed as she knew how to dress herself, appeared, certainly, not much above thirty-three or thirty-four.

The story of Lord Bent's engagement and marriage with the second Lady Bent was a rather interesting one. Lord Bent was wintering at Nice with his daughter Georgina, then supposed to be in delicate health.

One evening they were driving back from Monte Carlo, when a storm broke out. Rain came down in torrents, the lightning flashed, and the thunder growled. The horses shied at a railway train which was passing but six or eight paces from the road, and the driver, losing control over them, ran the carriage into a ditch.

Lord Bent and his daughter were lifted from the debris, shaken, but not very much hurt; and as return to Monte Carlo or advance towards Nice were equally impossible, they accepted the hospitality offered to them by Mrs. Canstrome, an American lady, who had hired a small villa close by, and was living there for the winter.

Mrs. Canstrome proved to be the widow of Judge Eben Canstrome, a well-known and well-to-do lawyer of New Orleans. She had come with her husband to Europe for the purpose of doing the regulation round of all the sights. Judge Canstrome had fallen ill at Rome, and had died there. Since then Mrs. Canstrome had lived quietly at Beaulieu, midway between Monte Carlo and Nice.

Mrs. Canstrome was exceedingly kind to Georgina, and more than attentive to Lord Bent. The earl and his daughter stayed at Mrs. Canstrome's little place for three or four days, and then the American widow, in her turn, stayed a few days with Lord Bent at the Villa Andato at Nice.

When the Riviera season was over, and people commenced to journey London-ward, Mrs Canstrome accepted Lord Bent's invitation for a fortnight to Farlowe Towers. Before that fortnight was over, Lord Bent had proposed to her. No doubt he thought that a woman like Lavinia Canstrome would look well at the head of his table; for, although her manner bespoke a certain uneasiness, she had about her that kind of polish which hides veneer and makes ordinary material look solid mahogany.

Mrs. Canstrome at first refused, or pretended to refuse, but in the month of June of that same year she had become the Countess of Bent. Georgina liked her stepmother very much, and to all outward appearances Lady Bent returned her stepdaughter's affection.

About the time when Mrs Canstrome became Lady Bent, Count Gyffa Brodie made his first appearance in London. He brought letters of introduction to the Countess of Bent, and from that moment forward the Count was a frequent and a favourite visitor at the Earl's mansion in Park Lane. Lady Bent said that he was a brother of a dear old friend, now departed, who had married a Roumanian nobleman, and had died at Constantinople. Most people in London Society at about that time were anxious to please the newly-made Countess, and with Lady Bent's recommendation, and those which he brought to other people of note, the Count's progress was easy.

As we have seen, there were persons, however, who did not take so kindly to the Count Gyffa Brodie as Lady Bent had done, and when I commenced to make my enquiries and tracked my Eastern nobleman home to his lair in Half-moon Street, and got to know what kind of men now and then came to see him, I began to think that dear old General Massinger was not so foolish in his surmises as people might have thought.

It was on the morning of the Friday after Lord Senfrey's murder, which had occurred on Monday night. Luigi Orano had been arrested on the Tuesday, and been brought before the magistrates on Wednesday. The police authorities had asked for a remand, which had been granted. The Coroner's inquest on Lord Senfrey and Maria Orano had been held on the Thursday, and both had been adjourned. The papers were full of the sorry business.

I was that very morning engaged in endeavouring to unravel the tangled skein of the Count's antecedents, when a tall and powdered footman knocked at my office door and brought me a letter.

"My dear sir," it ran, *"Lord Bent's secretary is out of the way this morning, and I have undertaken to supply his place. His lordship wishes you to call as soon as you can. This awful affair of poor Senfrey has so shocked him, and so prostrated Georgina, that neither of them know what to do about it. But Lord Bent thinks that somebody ought to take the matter in hand for Georgina and for him, and he wishes you to do so. – Yours truly, Lavinia Bent."*

Here was a combination both fortunate and interesting. I had often wished for the pleasure of Lady Bent's company, for the purpose, if possible, of eliciting an idea or two from her concerning her favourite Count Gyffa Brodie; but, of course, having once taken my place as a private detective, I could not hope for such a privilege except under unusual circumstances.

The unusual circumstances had arisen, and though I deeply regretted that the death of so good a fellow, and so brave a man, as Lord Senfrey should have been the means of obtaining the opportunity for me, I was glad that it had come.

I jumped into a hansom, and during the journey to Park Lane deliberated with myself about the position I would hold in this business. It was well enough to be instructed by Lord Bent, but I would have preferred that my orders should have come from

Mr. Martin Neymer, now his brother's successor, and Lord Senfrey. It would have given me a greater influence and a higher standing *vis à vis* the regular Government investigators.

But as I thought over it I satisfied myself that the matter was one of easy arrangement. I might, perhaps, be able to persuade Lord Bent to get the present Lord Senfrey to give me my instructions. They would open to me not only the mansion in Park Lane, but also the one in Eaton Square. The servants would give me their information with less restraint and with more sympathy.

Lord Bent's secretary, Mr. Oscar Hume, M.A., had evidently returned from his business when I reached the Park Lane mansion, for it was he who received me. I knew him, for he had been in the earl's employ some ten or twelve years, and I had met him years ago. He was a prematurely bald man, in the latter thirties, with a pale, sphinx-like, clean-shaven face, and strikingly cold grey eyes that, at odd moments, became impassioned. He moved with deliberate slowness, and always spoke in a low voice and with the Oxford intonation. I remember as a boy grinning at him, and receiving in return a look that quieted all my merriment.

"This is a horrid business, Mr. Grey," he said, in his slow drawl. "I suppose it will turn out to be one of those cases which the London police are unable to fathom. I beg you to be seated. His lordship will see you immediately."

As it happened, it was not his lordship who came downstairs first, but my lady, accompanied by no less a person than Count Gyffa Brodie.

Her ladyship greeted me effusively.

"So you are Mr. Grey?" said Lady Bent, holding out her hand for a second and withdrawing it again, as if remembering that I was a detective after all, and not for the moment Sir Patrick Grey's son. "This is Count Brodie, of whom, perhaps, you've heard."

I bowed in acknowledgment of the suggestion.

"The Count," added Lady Bent, "is the brother of a dear dead friend of mine, and he always advises me in matters of difficulty."

The thought struck me that moment that one might have imagined the proper person to advise Lady Bent to be Lord Bent.

"The Count thinks," Lady Bent went on, "that it would be wiser if Lord Bent were to give you a letter to the new Lord Senfrey. It will look so peculiar, he thinks, and I think, for you to be instructed by us, who, beyond dear Georgina's interest, have no position in the matter at all."

"What's your little game, my lady?" I questioned myself inwardly. "Do you want to keep me out of your house, or does Count Brodie suspect that I'm not as friendly to him as I might be?"

"That must, of course, be as Lord Bent wishes," I said; "but if you will allow me to offer a suggestion, I should say that the most suitable course will be for Lord Bent and Lord Senfrey to instruct me jointly. I should then report to Lord Bent and Lord Senfrey both, and would have the benefit of their combined experience and orders."

Lord Bent had entered the room by that time, and the old nobleman came to me as I stood up, and shook me warmly by the hand. He looked older than I had ever seen him, and all the twinkle of a smile was gone from his face. He looked into my eyes plaintively.

"So you're the little George grown to be a big man!" he said, still holding my hand. "They say you're clever. Well, help me in this. I'm not a revengeful man, but it makes my blood boil to think of poor Senfrey's fate. It has broken the heart of my poor child upstairs, and I want to be even with the villain who did it, if I can, for her sake. I heard what you said just now, and I think the suggestion is quite right. We'll drive over to Eaton Square together. Martin is there now."

I simply said, "Thank you, my lord," and bowed assent.

As my glance travelled from Lord Bent to the Countess and Count Gyffa Brodie, who stood a little behind him, I noticed a quick and savage look which Count Brodie shot towards the lady, a look full of meaning and angry reproach. The lady quailed under it, and a visible shiver ran through her.

"Hallo!" I said to myself, "what's up here? It's only a look, but there's more in that look than can be written in a page."

Chapter 3

Straining Upon the Start

When Lord Bent and myself arrived at Eaton Square, we found the newly-made Lord Senfrey and his wife busy in the drawing room. Both were dressed in black, and the lady especially made a brave outward show of crape and jet. She was too deeply engaged in the occupation of turning out drawers and examining knick-knacks to greet us with even a sign of recognition.

"My dear Martin," said Lord Bent, when he entered, "I need not tell you how grieved I am for the awful loss we have all sustained, and how much I feel for you."

Lord Senfrey looked round the room and towards his wife, and sighed; but whether the expression was one of weariness or concurrence in his lordship's remark no person might have told. My lady at that moment turned and returned in her fingers a diamond cross, which she had found in one of the secretaires, and paid no more regard to us than if we had been a pair of canaries.

"Poor Georgina is heartbroken," Lord Bent went on, and it must have been an awful shock to you – so sudden, so ghastly."

Lord Senfrey's shifty glance again flitted here and there, and he nodded his head twice and thrice in a half-dazed consent.

"That's simply too lovely, Martin," the lady exclaimed at that moment. "How your brother has been able to keep all these beautiful things I can't imagine." A magnificent *rivière* of diamonds and pearls was dangling from her fingers. "It will just suit me. I like diamond and pearls. This is much handsomer than the one Lady Hepdale wore at the last Drawing Room."

As she turned she espied Lord Bent, and nodded. A butterfly could not have exhibited less seriousness nor a sparrow less appreciation of the situation of the moment.

"You're getting on famously," Lord Bent said, rather bitterly. "Poor Senfrey's death means no loss to you."

The lady felt not the hidden sting.

"Yes," she replied, "it's an ill wind that blows nobody good. Now I have stepped into my proper position. When I was a girl I was told that I should marry a lord; and when I took poor Martin there for better or for worse my companions laughed at me. Now I have the laugh over them, you see."

I wondered within myself whether this nonchalance was real or assumed. If Lady Senfrey had been blind she could have taken no less notice of me. Yet she knew me very well. I knew her, and had known her father, Mr. Algernon Weyl, Secretary of Legation, before he died. Miss Agatha Weyl had been brought up in the shadow of southern Courts, first at Naples, then at Athens, finally at Rome. Her mother had been a Greek lady of noble birth, but bringing to her husband no dowry but her rare beauty, of which the flashing eyes were her daughter's only inherited legacy.

Miss Agatha Weyl's southern rearing, her intercourse with the men and women she met whilst still a girl, warranted no such cold-blooded indifference as she now exhibited. She had married Martin Neymer at a moment of despair, when a dashing and wealthy young Hussar had, for some reason or other hitherto unexplained, thrown her over.

Lord Bent shrugged his shoulders, and turned to the lady's husband.

"I've brought Mr. Grey with me, Martin," he said, "because I think that you and I both ought to have this matter thoroughly enquired into. The police are not always the best people for this purpose, and Mr. Grey, whom you know and whom I bring to you now, has at least the qualification of being a gentleman."

It was then that Lady Senfrey for the first time acknowledged my presence.

"Ah, Mr. Grey," she said, "you're there;" and she nodded.

Lord Senfrey again looked towards his wife, and in a weary, haggard way asked, "What do you think of it, Agatha?"

"Oh, bother the police!" exclaimed the lady. "I hate having anything to do with them, or with private detectives either. They're a great nuisance. They ask all sorts of questions, and want to know all sorts of things that nobody in the world can answer. I really wouldn't have one of them about the place for worlds. Poor Alfred is dead, and nothing that we can do can bring him back again, and there's an end to it. We'd better let things be as they are. No good can come of it."

"I beg your pardon," Lord Bent said sternly. "This can come of it. Poor Senfrey was foully murdered. He was about to be my Georgina's husband. I for one want to know at whose hands he met his death." Then, turning to Martin, he added, "You've taken his place, Martin, and it's your duty to do all you can to bring your brother's murderer to justice."

There was the same shifty indecision of reply. Lord Senfrey again glanced towards his wife, and haggardly said:

"It's a fearful trouble. What do you say, Agatha?"

"I suppose," said the lady, "I've got to put up with it. I don't believe in police or detectives either. They're a lot of fools. If they weren't, so many murders would not be committed without being traced. What's the good of employing Mr. Grey there? What does he know about it? He's an excellent dancer, and he sings very well, but he has never been a policeman – at least, I never saw him with a helmet on his head."

"This," I said to myself, "is put on. My lady has overstepped the bounds which distinguish natural callousness from acting."

In the same flash it struck me that, after all, Martin Neymer and his wife were the greatest gainers by the former Lord Senfrey's death. In the same heartbeat the ghastly idea shot into my mind – "What! can she have had a hand in it?"

Who could tell. She was known to be recklessly extravagant, and Martin Neymer was, everybody said, as near the bankruptcy court as a man can be without actually being gazetted.

"I'll think this over," I added in my mind. "If Lady Senfrey will only give me a trial," I suggested smilingly, "I will agree not to bother her with questions, nor to make my presence a bore to her. All I want is to be allowed to walk about the house as I like and where I like, and an introduction to the servants, which will ensure me their willing support."

"I think we'd better consent to this arrangement, Agatha," ventured Lord Senfrey timidly. "It will look better if we do. People expect that we should take steps to have this matter ferreted out. We must abide by the prejudices of the society in which we live."

"Oh, well!" cried the lady, "if it has to be, it has to be. And now I come to think of it, I've not yet had a look at the room upstairs where it all took place. Ring for Morton, Martin, and we'll go up."

Morton was sent for and appeared. The faithful valet was pale, and his eyes were swollen through nights of weary watching.

Lord and Lady Senfrey followed Morton upstairs, and Lord Bent and myself brought up the rear.

The former Lord Senfrey's own rooms were situated on the second floor. The door was thrown open, and we entered his sitting room and study – the chamber in which he met his death. The bedroom adjoined, and through the open door we could see the body lying there – the face white in death, and the wax-like hands crossed over the breast, as in prayer.

An old, white-headed retainer of the family sat by the bedside, and Sprat ran to meet us, and sniffing all round with enquiring glances at each person who entered, he slunk back into a corner of the bedroom and sat down there. Lord Bent noticed the little dog, and questioned Morton about him.

"Yes, that was his lordship's dog," Morton answered. "He's breaking his little heart over his death. He has barely touched food or water since his lordship" – the old servant stopped in his hoarse emotion and wiped his eye.

I had entered the room, and the first object I came across was the table at which Lord Senfrey had sat when he was murdered. The scene had been vividly described in the papers, and I could picture it all to myself – the box and the fiendish fumes that proceeded from it and enveloped their victim with a shroud of death. There was still a square mark on the tablecloth where the heated box had scorched the pile, and another one where a burning particle had dropped on to the cloth itself and burned a hole in it.

Lady Senfrey was standing by the open door of the bedroom, her gaze glued upon the corpse on the bed. The light from the window streamed upon her profile, and I could see her biting her lip and gasping slightly. Then she placed a dainty lace handkerchief before her mouth and approached the bed. Sprat jumped upon the bed in a flash, and stood there snarling and showing his teeth, as if intent to protect his master against further approach.

"Take that nasty dog away!" screamed the lady; and Morton, taking Sprat up gently, placed him beneath his arm, where the little dog struggled unavailingly to free himself.

"I won't have that dog in the house," said Lady Senfrey, returning to the study. "I won't be vexed by yelping curs."

"But that was his lordship's pet," pleaded Morton. "Poor Sprat didn't mean any harm, but his lordship used to spoil him so. He slept on his bed every night, and" – his voice had become broken and guttural – "if his lordship were alive, he would be very grieved if any harm came to poor Sprat."

"I don't care whose dog it is or was," retorted Lady Senfrey. "I won't have any yelping dogs about the house. I hate them. I'm always thinking of hydrophobia when I look at one. Don't let me see the little beast again."

Morton clutched the little dog closer to him and replied not. When Lady Senfrey had turned to say a word to Lord Bent, who had listened to all this in silence, I stepped up to Morton and said:

"So that was his lordship's dog?"

"Yes, sir," replied the man, "and a dear little dog he is. I don't know what to do about him. I dare not keep him myself. My lady might discover it."

"Oh!" I rejoined, "she'll forget all about it in a day or two, and then she'll alter her mind."

"No, sir, she won't," replied the man, and his voice sank to a whisper; "I know Mrs. Martin Neymer. She has a rare memory, and no more heart than a stone."

"I'm sorry for it," I replied to the valet. "You won't need to look far for a home for poor Sprat, and a good one, too – at least as good a one as I can give him. When you find that you must get rid of him, bring him to me, and I promise he shall be treated like a prince of dogs."

"Thank you, sir," the man replied with warmth, "thank you with all my heart."

I had been so interested in the case of poor Sprat that I had not noticed Lord and Lady Senfrey and Lord Bent, who were engaged in conversation at the study window.

"Yes, I do think it's an awful shame," the lady was saying. "He has left fifty thousand pounds – fifty thousand golden sovereigns – to that brazen woman, and Mr. Henderson, our solicitor, says that there's no possibility of disputing the legacy. Of course he had a perfect right to do what he liked with his money when he was alive, but I think that now he's dead it ought to go to those to whom it belongs by law."

"I beg your pardon, my dear Lady Senfrey," replied Lord Bent, with a grim smile. "It strikes me that it does go to those to whom it belongs by law. I suppose you mean to say that it ought to go to those to whom it justly belongs. But we all know well that the terms are not synonymous."

"I wonder," the lady went on bitterly, "how a creature like that Dorothy Anderson obtained such a control over Alfred as to cause him to put her name into his will; and Mr. Henderson told us that if Alfred had married dear Georgina that will would have been void, and if he had died only a day after marriage the hussy would have had nothing."

I listened with my heart in my ears. Here was another person who had benefited to a very large amount by Lord Senfrey's death. Dorothy Anderson was well-known to me by name.

It seemed truly strange to me that a man so skilled in the world's warfare as the former Lord Senfrey should have considered Dorothy Anderson worthy of being mentioned in his will. The girl was one of the brightest and cleverest actresses of the Sheridan Theatre, but from what I knew concerning her she had about as much heart as a mosquito.

And there was no doubt about it, had Lord Senfrey married Lady Georgina Rhowdon the will he had signed and the legacy it had contained would have been null and void. Was Dorothy Anderson aware of the legacy? Did she know that Lord Senfrey's intended marriage would void the will so made in her favour?

I have always held that a woman callous enough to break a man's heart without caring a rap what became of him – and Dorothy Anderson had done this more than once – was capable of any crime, if it suited her purpose. Social philosophers may scout the idea, and cite in proof of their reasoning the fact that very few murders can be traced to abandoned women, but my experience has taught me that if that class of people do not commit murder, it is generally because they are afraid, or because they can carry out their plans without overstepping the bounds of the law.

Given heartlessness and courage combined – and women are very often much more courageous than men – and given, also, the fact that the desired end can only be obtained by crime, I hold that a really heartless woman will not hesitate to commit murder, or, perhaps, oftener, to incite it, to gain her end.

For this reason Lady Senfrey's reference to Dorothy Anderson interested me greatly. I considered there was very little to choose in the matter of callousness between Lady Senfrey and Miss Dorothy Anderson. As far as that useful portion of the anatomy, the heart, was concerned, I thought them both equally deficient, and, as it had turned out, both were in their way greatly benefited by Lord Senfrey's death.

"You know very well, Agatha," the newly made peer ventured timidly, "why Alfred left the money to that girl. The will is clear enough. Alfred says plainly that he wished to provide for the woman whom, during a few days, he honoured with his undivided love. I must confess that I, for one, do not understand that kind of chivalry."

"I quite comprehend that you would not," Lord Bent rejoined drily. "Your brother's temperament differed so widely from yours."

Lady Senfrey bridled up at this retort. "Alfred was a fool," she exclaimed.

"Undoubtedly," was Lord Bent's quiet reply. "Most really honourable men are fools, to the world's thinking."

"Will you say, Lord Bent, that there was either sense or reason in Alfred's leaving fifty thousand pounds to the woman whom he himself acknowledges to have proved unworthy of his love?"

The old nobleman was incisively stubborn.

"No, my dear Lady Senfrey," he answered. "There was neither sense nor reason in it, according to the present acceptation of the word. In my young days people might have understood it.

Honour and chivalry were not quite dead then. Poor Senfrey was born out of his time. He ought to have been young when I was a boy. He was so old-fashioned in his conception of what was right, and so stupidly out of date in his ideas of honour."

"And yet," Lady Senfrey retorted, with a sneer, "they say that he broke that Italian girl's heart, and drove her to suicide."

"Who says that?" asked Lord Bent.

"People say it."

"Who says it? What people say it? Name them to me."

"Oh, I can't be bothered with naming them," answered the lady, driven into a corner. "Everybody says it. The papers say it."

"I beg your pardon, my dear Lady Senfrey," rejoined Lord Bent, with a look of quiet determination, "the papers would not dare to say it. That Italian, who is even now in prison on suspicion of poor Senfrey's murder, is the only person who has asserted it. But, before long, the mystery of that girl's death will be cleared up, and poor Alfred's assassin brought to justice."

The old gentleman uttered his words with a hot fervour, and looked so straight into Lady Senfrey's eyes, that I thought I saw her turn pale. But if it was so – and the light in which she stood was fitful and treacherous – it was only for a moment. I thought I saw her gasp and turn her head aside, and I looked on all the more interestedly. A little peal of semi-hysterical laughter answered Lord Bent.

"Of course, it will be all cleared up," the lady said. "I'm sure we all hope it will. Martin does, I know, and nobody can wish it more than I do."

I was standing in the open doorway of the bedroom at that moment, and as I casually glanced down I saw just behind the heavy plush curtain which framed the opening something white. I stooped and picked it up. It was a piece of paper a little over two inches long and about an inch broad, torn in an irregular shape from the sheet of which it had originally formed part. There were six letters upon it, written in imitation of printed characters – the letters "SENT FR – ."

"This room hasn't been swept, I suppose, since his lordship's death?" I asked Morton.

"No, sir," the man replied. "The superintendent said we were to leave it exactly as it was, and not to touch it by any means."

"Thank you," I said, and put the little piece of paper in my pocket.

Chapter 4

"Hinge and Loop"

Before I left Eaton Square I took Morton into my confidence.

"I suppose you were very fond of your master, Morton?" I asked.

"I shall never get another like him, sir," replied the man. "I would have gone through fire and water for him. I tried all I knew to save him; but I assure you, it was impossible."

"And I suppose," I went on, "you would be very glad if the man, or the woman, for all I know, who murdered him were brought to justice?"

"I would that, sir," Morton replied. "I'd give all I have – and I've saved up a pound or two – if it could be done."

"I think it will be done, Morton. Don't doubt that, though you will not be called upon to help towards it, except by your goodwill. I'm a private detective."

"I know that, sir," said the man, with a smile. "I've heard all about you, sir."

"Well, since you know it," I retorted, "it's all the better. I'm going to try and discover who is guilty of this awful business, and you'll help me if you can, won't you, Morton?"

"You may rely upon that," said Morton, determinedly and bitterly. "You can call on me early and late, winter and summer. I'd walk from here to Scotland barefoot if I could do anything to further it."

"That being the case," I said, "you can tell me the truth about one thing, because it will be of the utmost importance. Had Lord Senfrey anything to do with that Italian girl?"

"Nothing whatever," was the prompt reply, "I assure you, except introducing her to a theatrical manager, and lending her money."

"Of that you're sure?" I asked

"Quite sure," he replied. "I knew all about his little affairs. He'd no secrets from me, you see, sir, and he'd no more to do with that girl Orano than I had."

"You're telling me the exact unvarnished truth?" I asked; "hiding nothing? You're not thinking of shielding your dead master's character?"

"I'm telling the absolute truth, sir. If I were put upon my oath I couldn't say a different word."

"I believe you," I remarked. "Have you any idea how that girl came to poison herself, then?"

"None," was the man's quick reply.

"Do you know whether or not she had a lover?"

"That I don't know. I never saw a man talk to her except once, and that was one day when I took a letter to Miss Anderson at the Sheridan. You see, my lord got Maria Orano taken on at the Sheridan, and while I was waiting for the hall-keeper to bring an answer from Miss Anderson, I saw the little Italian girl come out, and a moment afterwards Count Brodie came out too, and they walked down the street together, talking to one another as if they knew each other quite well."

Count Brodie again. He evidently had the *entrée* of the Sheridan stage – a not very difficult matter, and not an occurrence upon which to found a suspicion of the crime.

"That was the only occasion," I asked, "on which you saw Maria Orano and Count Brodie together?"

"The only one," was the man's reply.

"Did you ever see Count Brodie speak to Miss Anderson?"

"He might have done so, for all I remember," Morton replied. "He used to be regularly at the Sheridan at nights during the short time my lord went there."

"Thank you," I rejoined. "Let me give you one bit of advice, however. Don't say a word about what you have said to me to anybody. It might get to the Count's ears, and it might prevent me from following out a clue I have in my mind."

"You can rely upon me," said the man. "I'll be as silent as a mouse."

"It's a case of *cherchez la femme*," I said to myself, as I was walking along from Eaton Square to the Sloane Square Railway Station. "A woman is at the bottom of it, that's certain."

Who was the woman? That was the question. I ran over in my mind the names of the ladies who were in any way connected with Lord Senfrey. There was Lady Georgina Rhowdon to start with, but naturally she was out of the question – one of the most lovable and loving girls on earth, pure-minded and simple, and always moving with a languor which by itself made crime and its attendant violence impossible.

Then there was Mrs. Alfred Neymer, now Lady Senfrey. She had been as poor as a church mouse two or three days ago. Now a fortune had dropped upon her as from the clouds. She was heartless among the heartless. Money was her god – not money for the love of itself, but for what it brought. She loved to fling the gold into the streets.

Could she have been the instigator of the crime or even the actual criminal? Her husband, weak, boneless, purposeless, was like an india-rubber ball in her hands. Such a woman, if driven into a corner, might play a desperate card and risk a crime.

Then there came three names, with all of whom, as I now found, Count Brodie was in some way connected. There was poor Maria Orano, whom Morton had seen in conversation with the Count. There was Dorothy Anderson, engaged at the theatre which he regularly frequented; and there was, last of all, Lady Bent, whose particular favourite he seemed to be, and over whom, I had little doubt, he had some kind of a hold.

I was turning these things over in my mind while I was seated in the railway carriage going towards Charing Cross. I was alone in my first-class compartment. It was one of those in which the partition runs nearly to the top and leaves an aperture curved above, and straight below, and barely a foot at its highest.

A sudden jar of the carriage, as the brakes were being applied when we reached Victoria, startled me from my thoughts, and I heard two gentlemen enter the next compartment. The train steamed away towards St. James' Park, and before I could fall into self-communion again my attention was attracted towards the men in the next division. One of them was a Scotchman by his dialect.

"Ah tell ye," he was saying, "et was just a piece o' luck sent to earrth from the sky for him. Ah'd a bill of his for twa thousand poon, and" – here the voice dropped a trifle, but as I listened attentively I could still follow it – "et was supposed to be endorsed by Lorrd Senfrey, and Lorrd Senfrey's signature was a forrgery."

"You don't mean to say so?" said the other man.

"Et's as true as the Gospel. Ah'd gi'en him tell the next day at noon to pay et, and the next day at noon he brought me the money and got the bill."

"You surprise me," said the other man. "I always thought Alfred Neymer to be one of the most honourable of men."

"So he 'es, ah've nae doubt," the Scotchman went on. "Et's that wife o' his. Ah tell ye, et just was a bet of luck for him, for ah'd told him that ah would prosecute him. Of course, ah would nae ha' done so en the end, but he didna know that."

Here was a discovery. Alfred Neymer had not only been over his shoulders in debt, as I knew, but he was actually threatened with a prosecution for forgery on the very day when Lord Senfrey was murdered. In such an emergency that wife of his might not have hesitated, and, placed between Scylla and Charybdis, might have fought for her husband's liberty by murdering his brother.

I sat still until we reached Charing Cross. There, as I got out, I looked into the compartment where the two gentlemen were sitting, and I recognised the Scot as Mr. Muir Macrae, the well-known money-lender of Duke Street. The mystery was darkening. It would require a great deal of skilful ferreting out.

When I got home, I took the little scrap of paper which I had found at Eaton Square from my pocket and examined it carefully by the aid of a magnifying glass. The letters had been formed by someone who used a "J" pen, for most of the side strokes were thicker than the up and down strokes.

The paper was smooth, stout, white writing paper, probably torn from a sheet of letter or notepaper. The quality was good. It was ribbed crossways, and water-lined straight up and down. One water-line was visible on my piece. I could find no other water-mark, except in one corner, where a little, nearly triangular mark was barely visible.

I looked carefully at the letters. They were formed by an expert writer endeavouring to disguise his or her identity. Some of the letters were exceedingly well-shaped, others were straggling, and certainly intentionally distorted. The first letter on my scrap, the letter "S", was such a one. It was a letter which a child in its first attempt to write might have formed. But the criminal had apparently lost sight of his or her purpose when making the last letter on my scrap the letter "R."

There the first up and down stroke was very thin, and the rounded portion at the top and the portion at the end were both made with vigour and self-assurance, for the loop was beautifully rounded, and the bottom of the "R" cut off sharp, showing that the letter had been made with swiftness and decision.

The writing seemed to give no indication either of a female or a male hand. I inclined towards considering it the writing of a man. But, then, I argued that very few men use a "J" pen in the manner that this person had used it, by holding it with the broad part of the point sideways.

"It is mostly women," I said to myself, "who use a 'J' pen in this fashion." But, of course, a woman might have written the words, and a man might have schemed out the horrible business with her.

I was thinking over the affair when my glance fell upon Lady Bent's letter, which I had received that morning, and which was lying on my table, and my gaze fastened itself upon it as upon a snake; for that letter, to be sure, had been written with a "J" pen held sideways.

I compared the paper of the latter with my scrap. There was no similarity. I tried letter after letter on my scrap with letters in her note. There was no resemblance, and of course there could be none except the similarity resulting from the writers of the two holding their pens in the same manner. But the fact remained – that diabolic scrap had been written with a "J" pen held sideways; of that I had no doubt, and Lady Bent wrote with a "J" pen which she held sideways. That was also patent to anybody who saw the letter.

My first business would be to obtain specimens of the hand-writings of all the people whom I suspected. For that purpose I wrote a short note to Lady Senfrey, asking if it would be convenient for her to see me on the following morning. I despatched this by express messenger. Then I sent, by my clerk Weatherby, a short missive to Miss Dorothy Anderson, simply asking a question relating to a friend, then in Africa, whom she knew.

In the first instance I was quite baffled; for the time, at any rate. Lady Senfrey sent her reply by telegram. My note to Miss Anderson came back, simply with the words scribbled in the corner: "Busy rehearsing. Don't know. Excuse scrawl. – D.A." That, of course, could give me no indication of what I wanted, as it was written with pencil, and most likely while the writer was standing up. I should have to try there again as well.

That same afternoon Morton brought Sprat to my chambers. He had combed the little doggie's long hair and had tidied him; and, in addition to his little silver collar, had tied a blue silk ribbon round his neck. He had tears in his eyes and could barely speak when he put Sprat down on my sofa.

"My lady has been at me again," he said, "about poor Sprat, and I thought I'd better bring him to you at once." There was a gasp and a break in his voice. "If my lord knew it," he said, "he'd turn in his—" He was evidently about to say "in his grave," but he arrested himself.

I went up to Sprat and sat myself down by his side and stroked him. The little doggie looked into my eyes coldly, but allowed me to go on without remonstrance. I took him up and put him a little closer to me, and he heaved a big sigh, such as a little dog is sometimes known to utter, and curled himself down by my side, looking up at me all the while; and after a little space of time he put his cold muzzle to my hand and gave one gentle lick.

This was, I suppose, as a token that he recognised me as a friend. To me it seemed that, if a dog could speak, poor Sprat said, "It doesn't matter what becomes of me now. My poor master is dead, and you can do with me what you like."

Morton had brought a little basket with biscuits and some chicken bones, and he spread them all out in a corner for Sprat to see. But the dog was not to be tempted, and remained on the sofa where he lay.

"You'll take care of him, Mr. Grey?" he said, half tearfully. "You will, for my poor lord's sake, won't you?"

"I will take care of the dog as if he'd belonged to me all my life. You can rely upon me for that," I replied.

"Thank you sir, kindly," the man said, and without a further word went out.

"There's a true servant for you," I said to myself. "If that man can assist me in my task he will – that I know."

Sprat and myself came to be great friends before the afternoon had far advanced, but, try what I might, I could not get him to eat anything. I had made up my mind to start my research that very day. Therefore I gave to my clerk, valet, secretary, messenger, and general factotum, Weatherby, all necessary instructions about the dog's keep and treatment while I might be away.

"I shall have to begin at the beginning," I said to myself; "and the beginning of all this trouble lay with that girl, Maria Orano."

I set out, therefore, towards James Street, Bedford Row. I was not long in finding the house in which the girl had poisoned herself. The number was 132, and it had the dark, dingy, half-squalid appearance of the regular Holborn lodging-house. It was an ugly, four-storey, brown brick building, totally guileless of ornamentation, the kind of house that abounds in the districts about Gray's Inn Road.

The windows shone like the surface of a stagnant pool with the dust and grime of months. The knocker on the door was rusty, the iron railings of the area suffered from a similar decay, and up in the regions near the sky at least two windows were mended with paper. In the sheet of glass over the doorway a time-soiled card announced to all and every of Her Majesty's lieges, and aliens to boot, that furnished apartments and bedrooms were to be let.

I looked round the street. It was of that semi-genteel respectability which covers a multitude of sins. In such a neighbourhood people of all kinds, classes, and nationalities would congregate. No clue whatever could be afforded from the exteriors of the character of the inhabitants within.

Nobody, it was true, might suspect that a nobleman or a millionaire lived there; but, at the same time, the occupations of the residents could be surmised only here and there from little brass plates underneath the bells. No 132 was neither much better nor much worse than its neighbours, and might have harboured a fledgeling Milton or a dying Chatterton, or, taking a more pessimistic view, might have concealed a murderer, or given shelter to a professional housebreaker.

I knew that the police would by this time have thoroughly examined the room in which Maria Orano had ended her young life; but I knew equally well that the late gleaner in the field of enquiry often gathers a rich straw.

I knocked, and the door was answered without much delay by a sallow-faced, elderly woman, dressed in the slovenly remnants of what had once been a decent cashmere gown, with a small black worsted shawl tied crossways over her chest and shoulders, and with her hands cased in ragged black mittens. A black cap, adorned with dingy blue ribbons, sat upon her head; and she kept one hand upon the latch of her door, as if ready to slam it in my face at the slightest provocation.

"And what may 't be you want, sir?" she asked gruffly.

"I see you've apartments and rooms to let," I answered very quietly; and the lady, thus peacefully addressed, relented, and opened the door a little wider.

"Come in, sir," she said, "and I'll talk to you."

I entered, and for a moment or two the passage, lit only by the glass aperture over the door, looked to me like a dark cell. The lady threw open a door at the side, and ushered me into a sitting room furnished in the regulation lodging-house fashion: green and yellow striped rep curtains, chair and sofa covers of the same kind, long faded out of recognition of the original colours, half-broken, cheap china ornaments, and mahogany furniture that had lost its lustre and, here and there, its regularity of construction.

"You must excuse me, sir," she said; "but I've been so bothered lately that I don't know whether I'm a standing on my head or my 'eels. Is it a bed and sitting room you want, or a bedroom alone; and is it for yourself, sir, or for anybody else? – not a lady, I 'ope, sir, because I won't take another lady in again, not if I know it; not if she was to pay me three pound a week. No, never no more – not while I'm keeping lodgings."

I admitted that I wanted rooms for myself, but I expressed myself to be content with a bedroom only. I knew very well that

Maria Orano had lived on the third floor, and to get into that room, or near that room, was of course my object.

"I've got a bedroom to let, sir," the woman went on; "in fact I've got two. One is nine shillings a week, and one is seven shillings; and if you don't mind coming upstairs, I'll show 'em to you."

I followed her, and was shown to a back room on the third floor, the one for which the lady demanded a weekly rental of nine shillings. From the description which I had read in the papers, I knew that Maria Orano had killed herself in the chamber opposite.

"Is this the only bedroom to let?" I asked.

The woman hesitated for a moment and then replied:

"You see, sir, it's a hard living one has to get by letting lodgings, and you look a respectable young man, and if you was to come and lodge here, I'd like to keep you. I don't like to 'ave lodgers coming here, staying for a week or two, and then go away, so I'd better tell you the truth, and the whole truth.

"I've got another room, the one in front 'ere, and I've been offering to let it for all sorts of prices, but I'm afraid I shan't be able to let it, because there's been a wretched girl living in there and killed herself – took poison; and the police have been 'ere, and the Coroner's officer has been 'ere, and Heaven knows only who's coming here next; and they've been worrying my life out, and asking questions, and put it all down on paper, so as I don't know what to say next and what I shall be asked next; and if you're not afraid of living in a room where a girl – and as nice a girl as ever you might have seen for the look of her – 'as been and killed herself, you can 'ave the room for seven shillings a week, and it's a cheap room, I can tell you. It's a front room, and nicely furnished."

"Very well," I said; "I'm not afraid of ghosts, and I'm not afraid of people who kill themselves. Dead people can do no harm. I think I'll have a look at the room."

It proved to be as pleasant a chamber as one might have expected to see in that house. Two flower-pots, which the dead girl had evidently bought, still stood on the window shelf, and the furniture-covers and hangings being of bright, if half washed out chintz, made the room look a little lighter and more cheerful.

"I think this will do," I said. "I'll take your room; and to make sure that you shall be all right and come to no grief," I added, opening my purse, "here's a fortnight's rent in advance."

The promptly proffered coin was probably sufficient evidence of my character as a desirable lodger, for the sallow-faced lady immediately volunteered the statement that her name was Matilda Rooney, and that her husband, dead and gone these ten years, had left her with seven children to support, and one of them a cripple that never could walk from its birth, and that she'd a hard struggle in the world to make both ends meet and get a hot joint on a Sunday; and that she'd be glad to know when I'd bring my luggage, for she'd have the room tidied up a bit.

How long the peroration might have lasted nobody might have told; but I stopped Mrs. Rooney's flow of speech by telling her that I had walked a great deal that day, and that, if she did not mind, I would lie down and have a short rest, and later in the afternoon I would sally forth and return in the evening with my belongings.

"Quite as you wish, sir," Mrs. Rooney replied, with an old-fashioned curtsey. "You've paid your rent for a fortnight, and for a fortnight the room's yours, though I do 'ope, sir, as you'll stay much longer, for all my lodgers, when they once come here, don't seem to be in no hurry to go away, though some of them do owe me a mint of money, sir, more as you'd ever believe any man with a 'eart in his body would owe t' a poor widow with seven children to support, and one of 'em a cripple from his birth."

I took off my coat and hung it upon the peg behind the door, and this movement seemed sufficient indication to the lady to take her departure.

"All right, sir," she said; "a wink with a coal hammer'll do for me. I'm off. You go and have your nap, and then go out and fetch your trunk in the evening. Good day sir; and pleasant dreams to you."

I was installed in the very room where Maria Orano had killed herself. I looked about the place, but of course it bore no signs of the tragedy that had taken place within it. I was about to go to the chest of drawers to open that, when the tramp of a man was heard on the staircase, and I stepped to the door and gently and noiselessly locked it. The steps approached, and for a second stopped on the landing outside my room. Then they passed on, seemingly, to the door next to mine.

I could hear the man try the handle. "*C'est moi,*" he said, in a quiet voice, the sound of which I seemed to know, and somebody within the next room rose, went to the door, unlocked it, and the man outside entered.

I could not hear the conversation, but the ring of that voice remained in my ear like the echo of one I had heard before. I crept to the wall and listened, but could hear nothing. After a while a slight noise reached me as of a man in the next room dressing. Then footsteps, this time of two men, could be heard on the landing outside. The men, whoever they were, went downstairs. I could hear the hall door slam, and then I stole back to the window and raised it, keeping my hand before my face.

After a few seconds I looked out guardedly. The two men were strolling leisurely along the pavement away from the house. The figure of one of them was quite familiar to me; but it was only at the next crossing, where they turned at right angles, that I recognised him. He was Count Gyffa Brodie.

Chapter 5

The Message From the Grave

Count Brodie seemed to be destined to figure conspicuously in my investigations. It was clear to me that he was on terms of close acquaintance with my next door lodger; and that being ascertained, the theory of an intimacy between him and Maria Orano was easily suggested.

Morton had asserted, and I had every reason to believe the truth of his statement, that Lord Senfrey took a merely friendly interest in the little Italian girl. Could it be that the person on whose account she committed suicide was Count Brodie? It was possible, but it seemed strange that if such were the case the police had no information upon the subject, and that my noble Levantine friend walked so unconcernedly in and out of the house where his victim had poisoned herself.

There was no time to be lost, and I immediately set to work to examine every nook and corner of my room. To start with, I went on my hands and knees and crawled over the floor from one end to the other. The carpet in the room was worn, and here and there torn. Underneath the bed the fluff lay half an inch thick. I noiselessly moved the bed, first on one side, then on the other, but could find nothing, except, at one corner, quite close to the wall, between the edge of the carpet and the wall itself, a little brass button.

I held it up to the light and examined it. It was a small button which had evidently belonged to a glove – a man's glove, most probably, from the size. That was not an extraordinary find in itself. I held it up to the light again, and found, in tiny figures, the letters "C.F. and Cie." stamped upon it. "That belonged to a French glove," I said to myself. "The word 'Cie.' tells me that. If it had been an English made glove it would have been 'Co.'"

I put the thing into my pocket and crawled on further. There was a little square table near the window covered with a greyish stained toilet cover. A little dressing glass stood on it, and there were various broken and unbroken little china trays and boxes belonging to an odd dressing table set. Just next to one leg of the table I found a single, thin, long, unbroken particle of Turkish tobacco. It was just one of the fine threads of tobacco that a man in making a cigarette might have dropped. That was not much either; but it indicated to me that either Maria Orano herself had smoked Turkish tobacco in the place – and Italian girls sometimes do smoke – or that somebody had been in the place who smoked Turkish tobacco.

I picked up my tiny tobacco straw with the utmost care and laid it gently on one of the little china trays, Then I searched for more. On another of the trays on the toilet table I discovered two particles of Turkish tobacco even finer than the first, and when I looked still further I found three or four more on the floor on the same side of the table. I gathered them all together carefully, and when I took out my magnifying glass I found that these were straight cut Turkish tobacco of excellent quality and crop.

I would have to question Mrs. Rooney about Maria Orano's habits, whether or not she smoked; and that would help me a great deal. Turkish tobacco of that quality was not sold in the purlieus of Holborn. It was patent to me that somebody had stood by that table and had there made a cigarette, and, as I opened one of the little china boxes on the table, my surmise became strengthened when I found there a burnt out wax vesta. I should have to learn if Maria Orano received visitors, and, if possible, whom. Another point of importance would be to know who introduced her to the landlady. After that I opened the wardrobe and all the drawers in the room. I turned out every speck of dust and left no corner where a pin could lie unexamined. But my search proved fruitless.

"Two things I shall have to find out," I said to myself – "to what kind of glove this button belonged, and where the paper was bought from which this scrap in my pocket was torn."

Twilight had been setting in in the meantime, and it was impossible to continue my search, as I was provided with neither candle, lamp nor gas-light. I went downstairs, therefore, and passing Mrs. Matilda Rooney, who, curtseying and grinning her sweetest, opened the door for me, I went out. My first journey brought me to the Strand. I dealt habitually for my gloves and hosiery at a shop near Charing Cross Station. I entered, and called the manager.

"Can you tell me," I asked, "from what kind of glove this button has been torn?"

The hosier looked at it.

"Oh yes, sir," he said; "that's easy enough. That's a French button, and the initials on it stand for Courtin Frères and Company. They've been supplying the market with a lot of suède gloves lately, and they've gone off very well – good quality and low prices. I should say that that button comes from one of them."

"Have you got any of these suède gloves?" I asked.

"No, sir," was the man's answer; "I haven't at present. We had six pairs, and sold them all."

"Do you know who is likely to keep them?" I continued.

"Oh, most shops in the West End keep them. If you look about Bond Street or the Burlington Arcade, you'll find them at a dozen places."

This was valuable information. A man had evidently been in Maria Orano's room who wore suède gloves. It would be my duty to know if Count Gyffa Brodie wore suède gloves.

From the Strand I strolled to the Burlington Arcade, and there, among the goods exhibited in the shop windows, I discovered at least three places where gentlemen's suède gloves were sold. While in the arcade I looked also into the fancy stationers' shops, to see if anywhere I could find a paper like that of my scrap. I entered one place, and putting out my little sample, without showing the lettering, I asked the man if he could give me any letter paper like that.

"Oh, yes, I can," was the man's reply. "It comes from an ordinary De la Rue eighteen-penny packet."

I bought my De la Rue eighteen-penny packet, and sure enough there was the same paper, ribbed, water-lined, quality, and all exactly the same. That paper was most likely sold by myriads of packets in London, and any one of the persons I suspected might have used that kind of paper. I felt a little disheartened at the discovery, but soon plucked up courage again. Many persons might have used De la Rue's eighteen-penny packets, but if I found that one of the people I suspected used such paper, it would yet be an additional step in my enquiry.

The Burlington Arcade was but a few steps from Grafton Street, Bond Street, where the present Lady Senfrey had lived up to a day or two ago. A thought shot into my mind at that moment, and taking advantage of it while the man was wrapping up my little parcel, I asked quite casually, "I suppose you've heard of the awful murder of Lord Senfrey?"

"Oh, yes," replied the man. "Shocking affair, isn't it? I'm very sorry for it for more than one reason. You see, Mrs. Martin Neymer, who is Lady Senfrey now, lived in Grafton Street, just over the way, and she was a regular customer of ours, and had lots of things from us."

This was news indeed.

"Oh!" I exclaimed. "I suppose she bought her stationery here?"

"Yes," said the man, "and lots of it – all kinds of paper, and all kinds of colours, and all kinds of shapes. You see that sheet there with "Agatha" in gold letters right across the corner of the page. We got that up for her. Now she'll move to Eaton Square, I suppose, and forget all about this shop."

I could not tell why, but as the man went on so carelessly the colour nearly faded out of my cheeks. Had I put my finger upon the right clue at last? Were my suspicions founded upon a shadow of fact? Had Lady Senfrey, driven to desperation by the threat of prosecution against her husband, resorted to this diabolic means of extricating herself from penury and Martin Neymer from prison?

"I suppose," I ventured, with a smile that must have looked sickly, "Lady Senfrey bought plenty of paper like what I've bought just now?"

"No," was the man's quick answer, "not much. It's a kind of paper that she wouldn't touch. All her own notepaper has some ornamentation of some kind – flowers, or gilt lettering, or something. Her husband, the present Lord Senfrey, might have bought some, but Mrs. Alfred Neymer – never."

At that moment a servant entered the place and asked for three packets of ordinary note paper, the same as "he had bought before," he added. The shopman handed him three packets exactly like the one I had purchased.

"That man came from a place that's closely connected with the Senfrey case," the attendant said, when the man had gone. "He comes from Rhowdon House, Park Lane."

"Lord Bent's house?" I asked, in amazement.

"The same," was the answer. "Lady Bent often comes here. We sell a lot of things to her and to the earl, and also to one of her friends, Count Brodie."

I am afraid the man must have thought me impolite, for I left the shop hurriedly, so dazed was I for the moment by the force of my discovery. At that early period of my career I was not yet so steeled to the exigencies of my calling as to be able to keep the thorough control over my nerves which I have since attained.

"There's no doubt about it now," I said. "Count Brodie has had a hand in the business, and the sooner I get upon his tracks the better."

But it was one thing to suspect Count Brodie, it was another to prove that he was guilty. I could not, at that moment, prove to myself even what possible advantage he had to gain, or what possible end he had to achieve by murdering Lord Senfrey. No crime is committed without a motive, and it would have to be my object to discover what motive he and Lady Bent, if she were mixed up with it, could have in taking the life of a man who, as far as I knew, had done them no harm, and through whose death they could not reap any benefit.

I rather regretted that I had not been present at either of the inquests, nor at the first hearing of the charge against Orano. I might have gathered so much by watching the faces and demeanour of the persons I suspected. Of course, when I first read about the business I had no inkling that I would be concerned in it. I was occupied with other important matters, and therefore paid but little attention to the Senfrey case. Now both inquests and the hearing of the charge against Luigi Orano had been adjourned until the following week.

After a short consideration of the pros and cons, I decided to take up my abode at 132, James Street, Bedford Row, for a few days at any rate. I returned to Craven Street and packed my oldest portmanteau with such articles of daily wear as I might need. Sprat looked at me mournfully as I moved about my room, and finally jumped on my little table and looked into my face inquiringly. He said as plainly as he could, "Please don't leave me here alone again." I patted him and stroked him, and he crept up to me as if he had known me ever so long. A dog's instinct is a wonderful faculty. Any decent dog knows a friend from a foe at a glance.

I gave full instructions to Weatherby, and, taking Sprat under my arm, I jumped into a hansom, gave my portmanteau to the man on top, and drove to Holborn.

I think I rose greatly in Mrs Matilda Rooney's estimation when she saw me arrive in a hansom, having evidently well fee'd the cabman, for he touched his hat to me with cheerful alacrity.

My portmanteau was not very heavy, but, with Sprat under one arm, I made a great show of dragging it into the hall. I had brought with me that which I knew to be an open sesame to the heart of ladies of the class to which Mrs. Rooney belonged. I had stopped the cab at a public house on the road and had purchased a bottle of the best unsweetened gin.

"Come in here for a moment, Mr. – Mr. – what is your name?" Mrs. Rooney said, opening the door of the parlour, when she saw me apparently distressed by the effort of lifting about fifty pounds. "Come here and sit down a bit, and then I'll give you a 'and to take your portmanteau upstairs. Nice little dog that is of yours."

That was just what I wanted. I entered the sitting room and sat myself down in a rickety armchair there. Sprat immediately took his post on the table near me, and looked at Mrs. Rooney with his head cocked on one side. The lady attempted to stroke him, but Sprat wriggled out of the way. Mrs. Rooney's breath was reminiscent of onions, and Sprat evidently resented it.

"My name is Grant. You'll remember it, won't you, in case of any letters coming for me?" I said.

"Oh, to be sure I will, Mr. Grant," responded the lady, grinning and curtseying. "I think we shall get on very well together, Mr. Grant."

I inwardly expressed the hope that the pleasure might be short-lived, but I rejoined, "I sincerely hope so, Mrs. Rooney. I give very little trouble, and even when I work at home you seldom hear me stir."

"And what may be your business, Mr. Grant?" Mrs. Rooney enquired, with a persuasive smirk. "Most of the gentlemen that live 'ere have something to do in the City. Are you in the City, Mr. Grant?"

"No," I answered drily. "I earn my living by spoiling paper."

"What's that?" interrogated the lady.

"I am a pretty fair draughtsman, and many of my sketches have been honoured by publication in papers comic and serious." In my little book there were two or three bits of which I was very proud. I produced them, and showed them to the good woman.

"Oh, that's it, Mr. Grant," she exclaimed. "That's very nice. You draw, then. And do they pay you money for doing that sort of thing?"

Mrs. Rooney's criticism of my artistic efforts was not flattering, but it was doubtlessly sincere.

"Yes," I answered. "It may be strange, but they do pay me for that kind of thing. It's very warm, Mrs. Rooney," I added, "and I'm very thirsty." I looked round the room. "You haven't a drop of – – ?" I asked.

"Not a drop," Mrs. Rooney interrupted me sharply, "if it's anything short you mean. I now and then do take something, but it's on account of my chest and my liver, and the doctor 'e says I ought to have a drop once a day at least. But I've been so poor of late and so worried, and what with my old man dead these ten years and seven children to keep, and one of 'em a cripple from his birth—"

I was afraid that the story of the lady's woes might be continued for some time. Therefore I produced my bottle from my coat pocket.

"I've brought this with me, Mrs. Rooney," I said, "because my doctor also has recommended me to take a drop now and again; and if you could find two tumblers and a drop of clean water—"

"That I can," the lady replied with gusto. "I always keep clean water – filtered water – and I'll see that the bottle in your room is always filled with filtered water; and if you don't mind waiting a second or two, I'll be up again in a jiffy."

Mrs. Rooney disappeared, and a moment or two afterwards returned with two tumblers and an earthenware jug full of water. The bottle of "Old Tom" was opened. I asked the lady to help herself, and she took a glass, and holding her broad palm in front of it, poured out about three-fourths of its capacity of the pure spirit. Then she filled up the small remaining space with water. I had noticed the operation perfectly, and could not repress a grim smile.

"I do hope, Mrs. Rooney," I said, "that my next door neighbour is a quiet man."

The lady smacked her lips, and having emptied her glass looked with greedy eyes upon the bottle.

"Oh, Mr. Byrne, you mean! Well, 'e isn't a bad sort, as men go, Mr. Grant," she answered. "And he's clever, if what I'm told is true. He's always inventing something or other, and always a saying that something or other is to make him rich, but he never does get rich. When I go into his room to tidy it, the place is chock full of things – clockwork things, and things like locks, and all kinds of queer things."

That was information to start with. Mr. Byrne was a practical inventor. That was worth knowing.

"Help yourself again, Mrs. Rooney," I said, pushing the bottle towards the lady. "Don't mind me. It's the best gin that can be bought, and it will do your chest and liver good."

Mrs. Rooney did not require to be asked twice. She helped herself to about a gill of the raw spirit.

"I've read all about your troubles since I've been here," I went on, while the lady gasped under the effect of the "liver medicine" and fanned herself with her apron. "I went and bought the papers on purpose. That poor girl must have had a lot of trouble. Have you any idea how she came to poison herself?"

"None whatever," Mrs. Rooney replied, in a more guttural voice than before, "as I told the coroner and as I told the jury. None whatever. I don't know no reason why the poor thing should 'ave taken her life, and she so young and so nice."

"Wasn't there some love trouble?" I demanded. "Did nobody come to see her?"

"Not a soul, Mr. Grant, not a living human creature soul."

"No man?"

"No man, nor woman, nor child."

"How did she come to you? Who recommended her?"

"Nobody recommended her as I know, except the respectable appearance of my 'ouse. She came here to look for lodgings, the same as you did and as anybody else might have done, and I'm only sorry that the poor young thing came to take away that which God had given her and which she couldn't restore."

Here was a new entanglement of the mystery.

"I have an odd question to ask you, Mrs. Rooney," I continued. "Do you know whether she smoked?"

"Smoked!" nearly screamed the lady. "That poor girl smoke? Of course she didn't. Why should she smoke?"

"I thought the room smelt of smoke," was my answer, "but I might have been mistaken."

"Then you are mistaken," Mrs. Rooney retorted; "I'm sure she never touched tobacco."

Then I was right. A man had been in the place, a man who smoked Turkish tobacco and who wore suède gloves.

I eventually left my "open sesame" bottle with Mrs. Rooney, receiving in return the good woman's blessings and the fervently expressed wish that I might often come and have a chat with her, to which I said "Amen" with mediocre enthusiasm.

She would insist upon helping me upstairs with my portmanteau, with the result that I had to drag to the upper regions an additional dead weight of perhaps eleven stone of alcoholic rebelliousness. Once arrived at my room, the good lady disposed herself in my armchair, as if intent to remain there, vowing that it was the sweetest room in the house, and that I was the nicest and most gentlemanly lodger she had ever had, and informing me, with tears in her eyes, of her devout wish that her old man, dead and gone these ten years, leaving her with seven children to support, etcetera, etcetera, might have been with her to see how a gentleman could behave when he was a gentleman, and promising that if I wanted breakfast at any time I should have all the soft roes in the house.

As Mrs. Rooney finally seemed inclined to fall upon my breast and to weep there, I yawned and stretched my arms, and began to unpack. Even this proved no incentive for departure, and how long she might have remained this deponent knoweth not, had not, on a sudden, a crash somewhere in the lower regions made the good woman yell.

"That's Jimmy," she said. "That's 'im who's been a cripple from his birth, that is. He's knocked my supper into the grate, that's what he's done. I know it. Four penn'orth of as nice tripe as ever you saw, Mr. Grant; and I think it's a shame for a poor widow to be left with seven children to support, and one of them a cripple from 'is birth."

I ventured upon the suggestion that if the tripe was to be saved from utter destruction by fire or flood, time would be the essence of the contract; and Mrs. Rooney reluctantly took her leave, showering upon my head more blessings than it ever could have carried in comfort.

When Mrs. Rooney was gone I locked my door, and after listening for a while and discovering no sound in the chamber next to mine, I proceeded to give another glance around my newly chosen apartment. It was a lovely moonlit night, and the silver rays fell dimly through the white muslin curtains upon the dark carpet of my room. They ran in mellow, glittering lines along the carvings of my mahogany bedstead and fell upon the bed itself in an opal patch. In the shade of the wall opposite my bed stood my candle, and the deeper yellow sheen mingled curiously with the pale light which streamed through the dingy panes. The old lace curtains on either side of the window looked to me like misty columns in the semi-gloom.

I gave Sprat some water, and tried to tempt him with food. He drank greedily, but I could not get him to eat more than a tiny morsel of a biscuit. I threw a rug over the foot of my bed, and arranged it so as to form a comfortable little nest for him.

I sat up for a while, and by the flickering light of my candle made my entries for the day into my diary, as was my habit. All the while I kept my heart in my ears, listening for every step, for every voice, for every breath. But next door to me there was no sound. If the man was within he was either asleep or as watchful as a weasel. I therefore undressed myself and went to bed. I had walked a great deal during the day, and with one thing and another, though not accustomed to retire early, I soon fell asleep. How long I might have slumbered I know not, but I was awakened by Sprat's movements on my bed.

When I rose to an upright position and rubbed my eyes, the moonlight was falling through the figured muslin curtains of the window, and the lacework threw little fantastic shadows into the midst of the greenish glow. It seemed to me as if the curtains were waving quaintly, and as if there was a flutter, delicate, soundless and graceful, among the lace. Sprat was sitting on his haunches on my bed, staring towards the curtains, now growling, then whining, now darting towards the window, and then shrinking back again, as in fear.

"What's the matter, Sprat?" I asked, pulling the little dog towards me, while he struggled and tried to free himself, his little body trembling all the while as in a fever. I looked around the room, but could discover no cause for Sprat's undue excitement, but he escaped from my grasp and again darted towards the window, and then cowered back again, whining loudly.

I looked again. I could see nothing but the peculiar formless movement which I had thought I noticed, like that of a human hand waved up and down behind the curtains, displacing the white, embroidered muslin strip, raising them and allowing them to fall into their natural folds again.

"What's up, I wonder?" I said, looking round with uninterested surprise. "You must really be quiet, Sprat. This won't do at all, you know."

I stroked him and patted him, but he would not be consoled. He stared as if his eyes were bursting from his head; and at last I jumped up, crying, "What can be the matter? Let me have a look."

Sprat had followed me out of bed, and darting towards the window had jumped on the window-sill. In endeavouring to gain a foothold on the narrow surface he brushed against one of the flowerpots that were standing there, and it came down on the floor with a crash. I picked it up, and as I did so a curious sensation fastened itself upon me, as if a cold, clammy hand were touching the hand with which I gripped the earthenware. I could not for the life of me have told why, but the contact seemed to be on me, and the moment afterwards I had to smile in spite of myself, muttering, "What a fool you must be, George! The next thing that will happen to you will be to believe that the ghost of this girl is haunting this room."

The pot had broken into two pieces on the floor, and the flower and earth, holding solidly together, were lying in one of them. In the other half something white attracted my attention.

I picked it up. It was one half of a sheet of notepaper folded together, and in it was wrapped a ten-pound note.

"Goodness gracious!" I said. "How does this come here?"

I examined the half sheet of paper in the bright moon light.

A woman had written on it the words, "Does he think he can buy my soul for ten pounds?"

Chapter 6

When Thieves Fall Out

THE man next door to me had been knocking against the thin wall which divided us, crying, "What's up, neighbour? Are you going to knock the house down? Can't you keep that dog of yours quiet and let people sleep?"

I could see nothing at that moment but those two pieces of paper in my hand, and had no ears but for my own thoughts.

"Are you hurt?" the man continued. "Can I do anything for you?"

"It's nothing, neighbour," I replied, at last. "It's only a flowerpot that has fallen from the shelf – quite an accident."

"That's a good job," the man retorted. "I'm dog tired, and I do hope you'll let me sleep after this."

I promised silence, but sleep after that was impossible to me. I put on my trousers with as little noise as I possibly could, and donned my slippers. Then I lit my candle, and went to the other flowerpot, and pulled out the earth and plant, but nothing was there. I loosened all the earth round the roots of both pots without discovering anything.

"That line tells its tale," I said to myself. "She was a noble-minded girl, and from what I know of Lord Senfrey he would not have deceived a girl of that stamp and led her to her death. No, that's much more like my friend Count Brodie."

I sat myself down and turned all the pros and cons over in my mind. The girl had come to the house without an introduction. I could see through that scheme clearly. Brodie had given her the number of the house, and told her to hire this room. He was evidently on terms of intimate acquaintance with the man next door, and thus would not have to ask for the girl when he wanted to see her. He would simply go up to my neighbour's room, and, once there, could visit Maria Orano without arousing Mrs. Rooney's suspicions, or, in fact, without anybody being aware of his presence in the girl's chamber. It was a clever arrangement, but just not clever enough to baffle anybody who enquired into such a matter with tact and decision.

As soon as the light was strong enough I crawled all over the room again from one end to the other. I noiselessly lifted the bed and the mattress. I carefully examined every nook, every cranny, every crack of a board. I raised the carpet where I could, and looked underneath that, but two or three particles of Turkish tobacco were the only additional trophies of my endeavours.

At about half-past seven o'clock my neighbour commenced to stir, and I could hear him dress himself. Directly afterwards I heard Mrs. Rooney come upstairs, knock and bring him his breakfast. I opened my door and reminded the good woman of her promise of the previous evening, and asked her to bring me up a cup of tea and some toast.

"That I will, Mr. Grant," she said, rather huskily, the best that's in the 'ouse, and something tasty with it, if you don't mind – something that you don't get everywhere."

"Don't take too much trouble, Mrs. Rooney," I remarked.

"And no trouble is a trouble, Mr. Grant," she retorted, "when it's being civil to a gentleman as knows how to treat a poor widow with seven children to support, and one of them a cripple from his birth."

I suggested that I was in a mood to devour elephants and digest snakes; and Mrs. Rooney's venerable slippers were immediately heard going pat, pat, pat down the stairs like a pair of clappers.

Mrs. Rooney was as good as her word. Not a quarter of an hour had elapsed when she returned beaming after the style of an undisciplined moon in a showman's booth.

"There," she said, taking the cover from a plate. "You don't get that everywheres you go;" and, true enough, on a piece of buttered toast she had spread three soft roes of red herrings.

I protested that this wholesale spoliation of the provisions destined for other lodgers was unmerited by myself. Mrs. Rooney, however, stoutly asserted that "there is herrings that's got soft roes, and herrings that's got 'ard roes, and herrings that's got no roes at all, and how are they to know what kind I've bought?"

Whilst Mrs. Rooney was standing by my table pouring out my tea with a smirky pride in her handiwork, I heard my next door neighbour go out and lock his door.

"Good morning, Mr. Byrne," Mrs. Rooney called out to him.

He rejoined gruffly, "Good morning," and went downstairs.

"There, now," said Mrs. Rooney. "He's gone, and won't be back till eleven. Then he'll stay here the livelong day until one of them gentlemen that he does business with comes and fetches him."

I listened attentively to the information vouchsafed. Mrs. Rooney's personality this morning wafted fleeting aromas of stale alcohol through the room, instead of the odour of onions of the previous evening. I had to bear the infliction of her presence, and to determine to draw some profit from it.

"Is Mr. Byrne's room nicer than mine?" I asked.

"Oh, dear, no," the good woman answered quickly. It was exactly the same as yours when 'e took it, but now it looks like a factory."

I asked whether it would be possible to have a look at it.

"Well," said Mrs. Rooney, "he'd kick up a deuce of a row if he knew it, because he's always strictly forbidden me to allow anybody to go into his room – 'not on any account whatever, Mrs. Rooney,' 'e says – and he can be such a bear when he likes. But you've been so nice that if you won't say anything about it to nobody, I don't mind letting you have a peep, though what you'll see in there isn't worth seeing, I'm sure."

I asserted that my curiosity was stimulated by what she had told me, and Mrs. Rooney, stealing on tiptoe to the door of the next room, as if the man were still within earshot, cautiously unlocked it with a key she had on her bunch, and we entered.

There was no doubt that the man was occupied in scientific pursuits. Implements of all kinds were strewn over the place, and portions of delicate machinery were lying here and there. A vice fixed to a table, and a formidable array of bottles and jars filled with chemicals occupied a shelf. What interested me most was the position of the furniture along the wall next to mine. I measured each inch of that wall carefully with my eyes. In the corner next to the window stood a wardrobe, but the cornice projected away from the main body of the structure, and between it and the wall a space of some five or six inches was vacant. Next to the wardrobe the wall was covered by hanging coats and other articles of clothing. After that came the bed, and then the dressing-table.

I had seen all I wanted. I thanked Mrs. Rooney for the privilege she had afforded me, and went back to my room. When Mrs. Rooney had left me – "for the best of friends must part now and then," I said – I locked my door, and immediately made my plans for fixing an ear trumpet to the wall.

The ordinary reader may not know what kind of an instrument is an ear trumpet such as I intended to use. It is a little tube of hard metal, and is made in divers lengths from six to eighteen inches. It is much smaller at one end that at the other, tapering from the size of a cob-nut to that of a pea. This instrument, when fixed in a wall with the broad end towards the room whence the sound proceeds, and the thin end projecting on the side where the listener stands, carries to the attentive ear every sound in the next room. It is only necessary to plug it with a piece of tissue paper to obviate the reverse process and the penetration of light. It is extensively used in the detective and secret services of most countries.

The only place in which I could safely insert my ear trumpet was in the corner near the window, where any tear I would produce on the paper in the next room would be hidden by the projecting wardrobe. I tapped the wall, and found that it was simply a lath and plaster partition. I took out the little pocket case of instruments which I always carried with me, and screwed my adjustable gimlet to the length of eight inches. I knew that five or six inches, at most, would be the depth of the partition, and so I found it. Guided by the sound, I managed to carefully touch the paper on the other side, and to pierce it without, as I felt sure, making an unnecessarily large mark. I then cut my ear trumpet to the length I required and inserted it.

"All's fair in love and war," I said to myself, "and, in the case of murder, any trap set for the villains is right and just."

I brushed away the particles of dust which had fallen on the floor, and then, taking Sprat under my arm, I went out. Mrs. Rooney bowed me out of the house as if I had been a prince.

"You'll find your room as nice as a new pin when you come back," she said, as she stood holding the door open for me. "I'll give it an extra lot of elbow grease."

I begged her to be sure and do nothing of the kind. I had arranged my belongings as I wanted them, I said, and I didn't wish them to be disturbed.

"As you like, sir," she rejoined. "Not as I mind the trouble, for nothing can be a trouble—"

"Good morning, Mrs. Rooney," I interrupted, with a doff of the hat which might have satisfied a duchess, and descended the short flight of steps. My first business, on my arrival in Craven Street, was to send a wire to Morton, asking him to call on me the moment he could. Then I opened my letters and gave Sprat, who by this time had apparently accepted me as his master, his breakfast. Less than an hour passed before Morton was in my room, and I went straight to my purpose.

"Can you tell me, Morton," I said, "if Lord Senfrey wore suède gloves?"

"Never," was the prompt reply.

"Of that you're quite sure?"

"Quite."

"Tax your memory," I went on, "because the point is of great importance. Are you absolutely certain that Lord Senfrey never wore suède gloves?"

"Absolutely certain. I know every glove that he wore. He used only Dent's kids and dogskin. I can show you every glove he wore for the last two months, because he never kept them for more than a week and then I had them."

"Can you tell me," I asked, "if Count Gyffa Brodie wears suède gloves?"

"I can't say, sir," Morton answered. "He might and he might not. I don't remember."

"This is more important in the cause of your murdered master than you can imagine. Do you think, Morton, that you can find out for me whether or not Count Brodie wears suède gloves, and, if possible, get me one or more of his gloves?"

"There's no difficulty about that," Morton answered. "I know Count Brodie's valet very well; and I've only to go to him and ask him to sell me some soiled suède gloves, and I've no doubt I could buy a parcel for five shillings."

This being arranged I strolled to Farquhar's, where I kept my tiny account, and where my father had kept his banking account for very many years. I had scribbled the number of the banknote in my book, and the manager immediately promised to trace it for me as far back as possible. Then I returned to my chambers and waited for Morton. The faithful servant soon came.

"I've bought all there was to be bought, Mr. Grey," he said. "Here's every glove Count Brodie has worn during the last month or so."

I unpacked the parcel, and, sure enough, nearly two-thirds of its contents were suède gloves. I examined the buttons. They all bore the stamp I had found upon mine; and as I went through them one by one I actually came upon a glove from which one button was missing. Probably it was the very glove Count Brodie had worn in Maria Orano's room.

In the course of the same afternoon a messenger from the bank brought me the following letter.

> 'Dear Sir,
> We have obtained the required information. The note C69935 was issued by the Bank of England, on May the second last, to the St. James' Branch of the London and Westminster Bank, and they in their turn paid it to the Right Honourable the Earl of Bent.'

How came Lord Bent's banknote into Maria Orano's hands? The answer seemed not difficult. The Earl had given it to his wife. Lady Bent had without doubt transferred it to Count Brodie, and my Levantine friend had used it to fee his inamorata.

Of course one might have enumerated a dozen cases, in any-one of which Lady Bent might have given the ten-pound ban-knote to Count Brodie in a perfectly innocent manner. The cause of charity covers a multitude of sins, 'tis said, and the note might have changed hands under its banner. The purchase of some article, the settlement of an account, and the like, might have been a reason. "That's not it, however," I said to myself. "That man's either Lady Bent's paramour, or he lives upon her. Either he blackmails her, or he's her lover."

I weighed the matter in my mind. The Count was a handsome fellow as men go – stylish, tall, straight-limbed. He had the ease and the polish of the French dandy, and well knew how to make himself agreeable when he desired it. Such a man might appear an Adonis to a hale and hearty woman in the early forties wedded to an old man.

"Poor Lord Bent!" I said to myself; "poor old man!"

And yet it was Lord Bent himself that I felt bound to make the keeper of my treasure trove. It would never have done for me to have kept the note. I knew that the police were extremely jealous of beginners in the profession like myself. They tolerated the old established opposition, but where they could put a spoke into the wheel of a new man they would certainly not miss a chance.

It would have been illegal for me to have retained possession of that note. Therefore I folded it into an ordinary envelope and closed that. Then I placed the whole into a second envelope – a stout, linen-coated one. This I sealed with my seal, and wrote on it, "Confided to the keeping of the Right Honourable the Earl of Bent. Not to be opened without George Grey's consent, except in case of his death." Then I took a cab to Park Lane.

Mr. Oscar Hume received me in the library. It seemed to me that he was even paler than usual, and his cold grey eyes moved uneasily, as if some trouble were on his mind. His passionless politeness still kept sway over him, but the nervous rubbing of the hands against one another betrayed anxiety.

"I do hope, Mr. Grey," he said, in his slow drawl, that you'll soon get to the bottom of this fearful business. The house seems turned upside down. Lady Georgina is very ill indeed. It's pitiful to see her."

I wondered in my mind why Lady Georgina's illness should have such a striking effect upon Mr. Oscar Hume. He was an old servant of her father, that was true, and as such he naturally felt the loss suffered by the daughter. But her husband might not have spoken more feelingly.

"You've come to see the Earl?" he continued, after I had seated myself. "I've telephoned to him. He'll be down in a minute."

He took his seat by his writing table, and the light through the high, open window fell upon his profile. It was a handsome face in its classic, statuesque mould. That was the face of an ascetic, of a student. I could not help admiring it. It might have served as a model for Ignatius Loyola. The curious thought had just entered my mind, "Is that man in love with his master's daughter?" but the moment afterwards, when I noticed the severe outlines, I said to myself, "No, that is the last of the passions to find a seat in that man."

Lord Bent came down, and Lady Georgina with him. There was no doubt that the girl had suffered terribly. Her big, languid eyes betrayed her grief. Her face was drawn and haggard, and she moved with painful deliberateness. She held out her hand to me with a sickly smile, and said, in a whisper nearly, "I suppose, Mr. Grey, it's much too early to hope for news from you?"

The poor girl's sorrow went straight to my heart, and if anything had been required to spur me to my task, the sight of her face would have done it.

"It is too early, Lady Georgina," I replied; "but you may rely that no time has been lost, nor will be lost."

"You'll do all you can, won't you?" she continued; "For my sake?"

"You may rely upon that," was my answer.

"We are all so glad that you've undertaken this business for us," said the Earl. "It seems to me as if our cause were in the hands of a trusty friend. You wish to see me?"

"Yes," I said, producing my envelope; "I want you to take charge of this. It's a document which may or may not be of great importance in this business, and I want to ask you to put it into your safe and there to keep it until I ask you to open it."

Mr. Hume rose at that moment and held out his hand; but I stepped straight to the Earl and gave the envelope to him.

"I shall be obliged, Lord Bent," I said, "if you will kindly take charge of this yourself."

Mr. Hume gave a barely perceptible shake of the head, and sat down without a word.

"I'll do exactly as you wish," rejoined the Earl. "Of course you've some reason for wishing me to do this, and for being silent on the subject at present."

"I have a very potent reason," I answered.

"That's sufficient for me," said the Earl, and put the envelope in his pocket.

Lady Georgina stepped up to me, and took my hand in both her own.

"You'll think of little Georgina Rhowdon, won't you in this?" she said fervently. "It's breaking my heart. They're accusing my poor dear Alfred of the most dastardly infidelity to me. Prove that they have lied, that he was the good and true man which I know he was, and I will be ever grateful to you."

I am not easily moved, but I felt as if there were a ball rising in my throat as she pressed my hand with her dainty fingers, and looked straight into my eyes, whilst hers were brimful of tears.

"I hope I may be able to do what you wish, Lady Georgina," I replied; "and tomorrow, perhaps, I may be able to say, 'I believe I shall do it.'"

Again a grateful pressure of the hand, and after looking back at me for a moment, she left the room with her father.

I looked round on a sudden impulse after the Earl's departure, and saw Mr. Hume sitting at the table with his elbow upon it, and his head resting upon his hand. He was staring at the open window. His lips were open, and his teeth hard set. There was a look of a brooding Caligula about him.

"That man's taking this matter very much to heart," I said to myself. "I shouldn't like to be Lord Senfrey's murderer and fall into that man's hands. I wonder if he is a Claude Melnotte, grieving for the sorrow of an unapproachable Pauline."

After calling at my office, and taking Sprat with me, I went to James Street, Bedford Row. I discharged my cab at Grey's Inn, and thence walked. As I came along the street, I noticed on the opposite side of the house two broad-shouldered, heavy-looking men, strolling leisurely up and down swinging their sticks. If they had been marked "Criminal Investigation Department" all over they could not have been more easily recognisable as ordinary constables in plain clothes. Another peered just round the corner at the next turning.

"Oho!" I said to myself: "They've discovered so soon that I'm here, and are watching the place."

The Metropolitan detective officers know well how to take advantage of the work of outsiders. The servants at Eaton Square and Park Lane had most probably been talking, and through them the Whitehall Place people doubtlessly learnt that I was engaged on this business. Their method was, therefore, after the standard regulation fashion. They were shadowing me. If my movements gave them a clue, they would use it or not use it, as it suited them. It was even better than their usual course, "from information received."

I did not mind at all. "The more the merrier," I said. My investigations so far had been of the most preliminary nature; and going, perhaps, into dangerous company, the presence of the Government force made me feel that in case of need I knew where to find assistance.

So I walked up the steps in front of the house with the air of a man who had been living there half his life. Mrs. Rooney had seen me from the kitchen and had run at top speed to open the door for me.

"Won't you come in, Mr. Grant," she said, "and have a rest and a quiet chat? It's so hot, and you must be tired; and there's still a drop left in the bottle."

I retorted that I was *very* tired, and that I preferred to go to my room and to lie down there.

"As you like," the good woman answered; "but you know you're as welcome to any place in my house as sunshine in May; and there isn't a thing that you could ask that I wouldn't do for you if it's in the means of a poor widow whose old man has been dead these ten years and left her—"

"Yes; it's a very sad story," I rejoined. "Good afternoon;" and I went upstairs.

Had Mrs. Rooney been less voluble, I might have asked her if my neighbour was at home, but now I had to discover that point for myself.

I went about my room opening drawers and shutting wardrobes and cupboards with sharp bangs, whistling loudly and singing staves of songs all the while. Between the snatches I listened attentively, but could hear no sound. Then, finding an old brass-headed nail on the mantelpiece, I went out on the landing and shouted to Mrs. Rooney for a hammer, which the good woman brought me. I prevented her entrance by holding the door ajar and showing my face only.

"I'm not fit to be seen, Mrs. Rooney," I said; and reached out my hand and took the tool, shutting the door again immediately. Then I banged the nail into the partition with vicious raps, smashing it in and pulling it out again about half a dozen times, until I thought that if my neighbour had been there he would have remonstrated against the proceeding. But there was no sound of any kind.

I therefore went to work to prepare for myself a comfortable seat by my ear trumpet. I had fixed the little instrument not quite four and a half feet from the ground. Therefore, seated on an ordinary chair, my ear was just on a level with the tiny aperture. I placed the hearthrug on the floor, so that part of it stood up against the wall. On that I put a cane-seated chair, trying it first of all to assure myself that it did not creak. Over that again I threw my rug. Then I took off my shoes, and didn't even resume my slippers, but sat down in the corner with my ear to the trumpet.

No sound of any kind could I hear. There was no question about it – my neighbour was not within.

On that spot I sat nigh on an hour before a knock at the door below and a banging of it, and steps coming upstairs, announced to me the advent of Mr. Byrne and of another. Then I heard a slight push against my door, and the creaking of the boards, as if somebody were trying to discover if the door were locked. A moment afterwards the two men entered the next room. I kept my ear to my trumpet for dear life. They were talking in French, which I understood perfectly.

"He is not there," said one voice, in a hoarse whisper, which I recognised as that of my neighbour.

"Do not make so sure of that," said the other, unquestionably Brodie's, even more cautiously than his companion's. "Those men walking up and down outside are policemen. That man next to you may be a policeman also."

"Do not be a fool," said the other. "You suspect everybody and everything. I tell you I asked that old woman downstairs. He is a draughtsman. She saw his sketches."

"Very well, then, since you will have it so; but that is no reason why you should shout like that."

Their voices dropped to a lower pitch than before, but I could still hear them plainly.

"Now," continued Count Brodie, having evidently seated himself, as I heard the movement of his chair, "I want to get away from here as soon as I can. I have to dine at Lord Sleyburne's at seven, and after that I am going to a ball."

"Good," said the other, "I do not want your company. Have you brought what I asked you?" There was a pause of a few moments. "You have had three hundred pounds from me in the last month," replied Brodie.

"Yes," said the other, "I had it, and I have it no more. It has all gone to the patent agents, and to the stockbrokers. I lost over one hundred pounds on Egyptians because I had not the money to give a cover to buy in time. I only want two hundred pounds now."

"Yes," answered Brodie, "two hundred pounds! You speak as if they were two hundred centimes. You are not satisfied with those cursed patents of yours, that cost hundreds and never bring in a farthing. You must gamble on the Stock Exchange and squander fortunes, and yet you live in this hole, like a beggar. I tell you I can't continue it. I have had to pull in my horns lately. I have had to lose money to divert suspicion. It is not like last year, when I could haul in three and four hundred pounds a night. I dare not win much just now, and I must lose now and again."

"What is that to me?" retorted the other. "It is not necessary that you should win to be able to get me two hundred pounds. Ask your wife to give you the money."

"She has given me all she could, and it might be dangerous to ask for more."

"Rubbish!" was the rather louder rejoinder. "If I had a wife whose husband is a millionaire earl, I would very soon make her give me what I wanted." I thought my heart was standing still as I listened to the words.

"I tell you," replied Brodie, and his words sounded like savage hisses, "*she* cannot do it, and *I* cannot do it."

"And I tell you," Byrne went on, "that *she will* have to do it, and *you will* have to do it."

"It is a threat, then?" asked Brodie.

"Yes, it is a threat. When a man has a wife who at the same time is the wife of a British earl, and he cannot lend two hundred pounds to help a friend, he must be made to do it. Will you get it from her, or shall I go to her and say that I will tell her husband that Lady Bent is not his wife, but the wife of Bernard Clankton, formerly a Parisian gambling-house keeper, sent to penal servitude for robbery and attempted murder, and supposed to have died in New Caledonia? How would a rumour that you are not

Count Brodie, but that same Bernard Clankton, escaped from the galleys, suit your cards?"

There was a silence of a few heartbeats' space in the next room, during which a man might have heard a fly walk on the wall. Then I could hear Brodie's remark: "So you would do this?"

"Yes," was the whispered hiss.

"Then you would have to confess that you yourself are a returned convict."

"Oh!" said the other, "it is different with me. I was discharged. I am free. But you they can take back, and make you serve out the remainder of your sentence."

There was another pause, during which I could hear the furious tapping of Brodie's foot on the floor.

"And what else would you tell then?" the Levantine asked, at last.

"That I cannot say at present," was the rejoinder. "It depends."

"You hound!" snarled Brodie.

"As you please," retorted the other quietly; "but I want two hundred pounds."

"I have not got them now."

"Let me see," was the reply. "It is Saturday. The banks are closed. They will reopen on Monday at ten. I will give you till Monday at two to get them."

"And then, if I do not bring them?"

"Then I will take what steps I shall decide upon."

"All right," exclaimed Brodie; and without a further word he went to the door, unlocked it, and I could hear him go downstairs.

I sank back in my chair.

Chapter 7

Recorded Time

I NEVER let the grass grow under my feet; and having consigned Sprat to the special care of my man-of-all-service, Weatherby, I travelled on that same Saturday night to Paris. I arrived there in the early morning, and went to a comfortable little hotel in the Rue Laffitte, where I generally take up my quarters when in the capital of sunny France.

When I first started in business as a detective, I had placed myself in communication with men engaged in the same profession all over the world. My Paris correspondent lived in the Rue Bleue, a short street leading out of the Rue Lafayette

Sunday is not held as sacred in Paris as it is in London, and after my usual morning tub and a hearty breakfast, in which the English and the French methods mingled in agreeable and substantial variety, I walked to the Rue Bleue. My correspondent, Monsieur Achart, a thin and lithe little man, with fierce, stubby moustache, piercing eyes, and the quietest possible manner ever known in a Frenchman, received me cordially.

"It is a miracle," he said, "to see you in Paris, Monsieur Grey. I am enchanted. You come on business, of course?"

I admitted the impeachment.

"I want you to help me, Monsieur Achart," I said. "You have sufficient influence, I suppose, at the Prefecture to get me the dossiers of a couple of persons today?"

For the information of those of my readers who are not conversant with French legal procedure, I will state the following. In France, a record is kept officially of the doings and misdoings of every Frenchman and, as far as possible, of every foreigner domiciled in France. The moment a Frenchman is born, and his birth is registered, his dossier, that is to say his record, is commenced, and thenceforth kept.

If there are no entries on the dossier, it is called "blank," and that means it is that of an honest man. But any slight difference of opinion with the authorities and contravention of the law, and especially any charge made against a citizen, and any conviction, is immediately recorded.

This dossier is especially used against prisoners brought up for their trial, and in the case of such prisoners, whether they be Frenchmen or foreigners, it is especially exhaustive. The police make the fullest possible enquiries, and search out the story of the subject's existence, to leave it inscribed for ever in the archives of the French police.

I knew, from what I had overheard on the previous afternoon, that the dossier of Bernard Clankton, alias Count Gyffa Brodie, and of his wife, now called Lady Bent, would exist in full at the Paris Prefecture of Police, and that my friend Monsieur Achart would most likely be able to obtain a copy of it for me on that very day, Sunday though it was.

"Of course I have," answered the little Frenchman. "Let me have the names, and you shall not have long to wait."

I gave him the names, Bernard Clankton and his wife; adding that I did not know the Christian name of the lady.

"Bernard Clankton? Bernard Clankton?" he repeated. "Yes; I know that name well. He kept a gambling den in the Rue du Mont Thabor, where he fleeced everybody, English and Americans especially. He had a handsome wife, whom he used as a decoy, and the fool was doing well, but then robs and nearly murders an old Brazilian. They arrested him at Havre, on board of one of the steamers, and brought him back, he was sentenced to the galleys."

"Do you know anything about his wife?" I asked.

"I saw her once or twice," Monsieur Achart answered. She was a lovely woman – tall, and of the English type. She seemed to me to be always half in tears, and I pitied her."

"Those are the two people," I said, "whose dossiers I want."

"Very well," answered my correspondent. "I suppose, as you have come on business only, you want to go back tonight?"

"I do," was my reply.

"Very well; you shall lunch with me at Vian's, in the Rue Daunou, an old-fashioned place, where they give you something to eat that is fit to be eaten. I will bring you the copies of the dossiers; and if I cannot get copies of them today, I will arrange that they shall be forwarded to you direct to London. After that you can spend the afternoon with me, and go back this evening."

That was exactly what I wanted; and the little man was as good as his word. I met him at two o'clock at Vian's.

"I have had some trouble over this," he said. "My friend Amadeu, at the Prefecture, was away, and the officer on duty was not so easily persuaded. Still, he knew that I was a great friend of his colleague, and I told him that I would render him any service in return. So here are the documents, duly copied out and attested."

He handed me the two papers, and I merely glanced at them for a second, to assure myself that the right persons were therein described, and then put them in my pocket. We passed the afternoon agreeably; and that same night the express bore me back to London. I had plenty of time to read my two precious sheets of paper. The documents were lengthy, and portrayed minutely the life's incidents of both, and I give here the more important entries:

CLANKTON (BERNARD ROSILIO)

1845. Feb. 28. – Born at Gaeta, Malta. *Father*, Humphrey Clankton, Private Royal Engineers, English Army, Protestant. *Mother*, Rosa Rosilio, laundress, Catholic.

1851. May 17. – Father left Malta for Gibraltar.

1853. Bernard at School, Franciscan Fathers. 1853. Dec. 11. – Convicted, theft.

1854. Mother moved to Paris.

1854. Bernard at School, Brotherhood of Jesus.

1854. Sept. 2. – Expelled for theft.

1858. Oct. 3. – Convicted, theft. Six weeks' imprisonment.

1859. Jan. 11. – Convicted, obtaining money by fraud. Two months' imprisonment.

1859. June 2. – Convicted, theft with violence. Two years' imprisonment.

1862. April 18. – Mother died; left 11,562 francs to Bernard.

1864. Bernard accused of robbery of Englishman. Acquitted.

1867. Bernard, in company with Jasper Byrne (*alias* Jasper Hunter), mechanical engineer, sets up gaming house at Rue Montaigne, 114.

1868. Many complaints; house watched

1869. Jan. 1 – House closed.

1869. Feb. 12. – Bernard and Byrne convicted. Bernard nine months' imprisonment.

1871. Jan. 6. – Bernard and Byrne set up gaming house Rue du Mont Thabor, 163.

1872. Feb. 10. – Bernard marries Lavinia Meredith, aged twenty-two, spinster, English.

1880. Mar. 17. – Bernard, Byrne and Lavinia accused of robbery and attempted murder. Lavinia acquitted; Bernard convicted, ten years' transportation; Byrne, three years'.

1884. June 3. – Was drowned on beach at New Caledonia.

MEREDITH (LAVINIA).

1850. Mar. 10. – Born Ivybridge, Devonshire, England. *Father*, Geoffrey Meredith, gentleman farmer, Protestant. *Mother*, Ellen Meredith, his wife, Protestant.

1859. April 7. – Father was killed in railway accident.

1859. April 9. – Mother died, after premature confinement.

1867. May 11. – Came to Paris as governess.

1868. English governess at school, No. 2, Avénue Milton, Vénery Sœurs.

1872. Feb. 10. – Marries Bernard Rosilio Clankton.

1880. Mar. 17. – Accused complicity in robbery and attempted murder. Acquitted.

1885. Dec. 4. – Marries Eben Canstrome, judge, New Orleans, United States of America.

1890. Jan. 3. – Eben Canstrome dies at Rome.

1891. Sept. 10. – Marries the Earl of Bent, London.

As I read the two papers over and over again, and the story of Lady Bent lay revealed to me in all its pitiful nakedness, I could not help feeling sorry for the poor woman. I could read between the lines of that fierce and graphic document the story of a life of misery. The father dead when she was but a child, and the mother following him to the grave but a few days afterwards.

I could imagine the drudgery of that establishment in the Avénue Milton, and the artifices of the smooth-tongued villain, who saw in the handsome English girl a suitable decoy for his gaming house, and who married her, probably, simply because he needed her for a tool. Had she been aware of the fact that her first husband was alive when she married Judge Canstrome; and afterwards, again, when she married the Earl?

What a well-spring of sorrow and shame would pour its flood upon that good old man when the whole miserable scandal became public! It was sure to become public, I thought. I myself saw no way of staying my tongue. That Maltese scoundrel had laid his plans well; but I knew enough about him now to satisfy General Massinger.

I deliberated with myself whether I should speak at once, or whether delay was the wiser course. I had learnt much, but as yet I had no proof whatever which could connect any of the persons I suspected with the mystery I was commissioned to unravel – the murder of Lord Senfrey. I had advanced far enough in my research to fully clear Lord Senfrey's memory. But that was not discovering his murderer.

But now, of course, I could see a reason why Lady Bent and Gyffa Brodie should devoutly wish for Lord Senfrey's death. The motive was easily surmised. If, by any means whatever, Lord Senfrey had become aware of Lady Bent's bigamy, and of her relations with her first husband, she and Brodie might have combined to silence his tongue by poison.

"No," I said to myself; "we must wait. We must be patient, and keep on the same road."

On my arrival at Victoria that morning, I took a cab straight to James Street, Bedford Row.

Mrs. Rooney was engaged in cleaning the steps which led to her front door. She looked at me with open eyes and mouth agape, as I jumped from the vehicle. A great black smudge ran across her sallow cheek and forehead. Her little black lace cap obscured one eye, and she attempted to dislodge it by various upward puffs of breath, but it remained refractory.

"So you've come back, at any rate, Mr. Grant," she said, looking at me as if she were half dazed. "That's a good job."

"Of course I've come back, Mrs. Rooney," I replied. "Why shouldn't I? Has anything upset you?"

"Upset me?" she retorted. "It's enough to drive a poor woman crazy. There's been you not coming home these two nights, and there's been Mr. Byrne, who went away only a few minutes after you did on Saturday night, and he hasn't been back ever since; and three or four gentlemen have been here swearing as they knew he was at home, because he said he'd be at home; and him not coming near the place."

I could feel my heartbeat against my ribs as I heard the news. Jasper Byrne had not slept in his room either on the Saturday or the Sunday night. This very day at two o'clock Gyffa Brodie was to bring him two hundred pounds. Had Gyffa Brodie removed from his path another person possessed of dangerous knowledge concerning him?

"Oh! I often stay away for two or three nights," I said, in a tone of perfect commonplace. "I've friends all over the country. You must never trouble about me."

Mrs. Rooney gave another unsuccessful puff at her rebellious cap, and looked at me pitifully.

"I've been so worried, Mr. Grant," she said, half tearfully. "First of all it's that girl that kills herself, and the policemen ransacking the place, and the coroner and the jury and the lawyers wanting to know things that how anybody is to know them is a puzzle. Then it's you and Mr. Byrne as stays away for two nights; and first one gent comes and says he knows that Mr. Byrne is in, and won't take no for an answer; and then another, and another, all asking questions, and wanting to see for themselves; and what's a poor widow to do whose old man has been dead these ten years—"

"I can sympathise with you, Mrs. Rooney," I said. "I also had a relative, a dear old grandmother, who has been dead these fifteen years."

"Has she?" guilelessly questioned Mrs. Rooney. "Poor old lady!"

"Are you quite sure that Mr. Byrne hasn't been home?" I asked. "Have you looked into his room?"

"Of course I have," she replied. "I haven't slept a wink, and I'm half dead, that I am."

I hinted that the word "breakfast" had an attraction for me at that moment; and the good woman scrambled along the passage and down her kitchen stairs, fiercely fighting her rebellious cap, and crying all the while,

"What a fool I am! Of course you want breakfast, Mr. Grant, of course you do;" and disappeared somewhere in the lower regions.

I had looked up and down the street when I arrived, without seeing anybody whom I could recognise as a policeman in plain clothes watching the house; but when I carefully lifted the little-short curtain of my window and peered out, I saw right opposite to me, on the second floor of the house facing Mrs. Rooney's, two bearded faces, with their eyes fastened upon my window.

The men were standing behind their curtain in a clumsily cautious manner; but a minute or two afterwards one of them left the house, and walked up and down the street. I saw the police constable on the beat stroll leisurely past him with his hands behind his back. My burly, bearded friend seemed to brush against him, and I saw a quick movement of the arm towards the constable's two hands, which were still behind his back. My bearded friend had no doubt passed a paper of some kind to the policeman on duty. The latter strolled on as if nothing had occurred, and as if he had seen nobody.

"That's a communication for Whitehall Place," I said. "In a quarter of an hour they'll know that I've returned from Paris."

Lord Senfrey's remains were to be conveyed that morning to Paddington Railway Station, to be taken for interment to a little God's Acre near Swindon, where his father and mother slept in peace. In his will he had expressed a wish that, having passed so much of his life amid the turmoil and strife of this world, he might be interred in that secluded hamlet.

I should have liked to have gone to Paddington, but I had to choose between any results I might obtain from watching the faces there and the possibility of the chances that might arise to me at Mrs. Rooney's house. I preferred the latter, and decided to remain.

"Who lives in the house opposite to you?" I asked Mrs. Rooney, when she brought me my breakfast.

"The one across the way, you mean?" said the woman, "the house with the brown curtains and the brass knocker?"

I nodded in the affirmative.

"That's Mrs. Garrison what lives there. Her husband was a policeman – an inspector. She lets lodgings the same as myself. She wasn't doing much until a couple of days ago. Now there's two or three gentlemen that lives there."

I asked Mrs. Rooney if any of Mrs. Garrison's lodgers had been asking her questions, and the good woman answered, "No; I've had enough of that kind of thing from them as has a right to ask."

The Whitehall Place people were evidently determined to shadow me.

"Very well," I said to myself; "let them. I can keep my counsel all the same."

I waited in my room until two o'clock, but not a soul came. Byrne did not return, and Brodie did not call. I listened for every sound on the stairs, for every opening of the door below, for every voice at the door. Only one man called for Byrne, but he went away again; and as I watched him going down the street, I saw that it was not Brodie.

Another hour – till three o'clock. Still nobody. I got Mrs. Rooney to bring me my luncheon, and pretended to be busily engaged in drawing. Another hour. I waited until the hands of my watch pointed to four. Still nobody.

"I'm afraid it's all over with poor Byrne," I said to myself. "His body will be found in the Thames, or in some out-of-the-way corner. That Brodie would have called if he were not fully cognisant of whatever misadventure has befallen his former companion in crime."

I picked up my hat and walked out, and soon discovered that I was honoured by the distinguished company – at a respectful distance, it was true – of two members of the Criminal Investigation Department.

I went straight to my office, and there found Sprat, who seemed to be in the seventh heaven of joy at seeing me again, he crawled up to me, and whined, and wagged his tail, and barked, as if delighted beyond measure. The poor doggie no doubt thought that he had lost me, as he had lost his former master. I sent Humphrey for Morton, while I ran over my correspondence, and I had barely finished my letters when the faithful valet came.

"Can you tell me, Morton," I asked him, "if your master ever had a quarrel with Lady Bent?"

"Not that I know, sir," replied Morton; "not an open quarrel, because I should have known that. But he didn't like her, that I know; and one night I heard him call her 'that awful woman.'"

"When was that?" I asked.

"It was just after he and Lady Georgina had become engaged," Morton answered. "My lord, I think, found out something about Lady Bent that didn't please him; and Lady Bent called upon him, and they were together for a long time in the drawing room, and when Lady Bent came out my lord was paler than I've ever seen him before. But there had been no quarrel, I know, for not a sound of their voices could be heard in the ante-room. My lord was one of those men who knew how to keep his counsel when he wanted to, although he had few secrets from me; and he never referred to the call of Lady Bent, so I don't know what it was about."

"Thank you, Morton," I said; "that's all I wanted to see you about for the present."

Had Lord Senfrey discovered the fact of Lady Bent's bigamy, and had he in his generous nature consented to spare her, or rather, to spare her poor husband and his delicate daughter? That was a vital question. The vacillating finger of doubt pointed to the affirmative side.

I was anxious to return as speedily as possible to Mrs. Rooney's hospitable roof, and therefore, taking up Sprat, I jumped into a hansom and drove to Holborn.

I found Mrs. Rooney as haggard and as anxious as before. In reply to my question whether anybody had called for me or whether she had seen her lodger, she answered, with a mute shake of the head, looking at me all the while as if she would dearly have liked to cry.

"I know there'll be another inquest," she said; "I know it. It can only happen to a poor woman like me, that's a widow, whose old man has been dead these ten years—"

"Oh, don't speak of such things, Mrs. Rooney!" I interrupted. "Mr. Byrne will turn up all right – tonight, most probably."

"Not he," she answered, "not he. He'd have told me if he'd intended to stay away of his own accord. He always did. He was that regular that Big Ben's a sham to him. Something's wrong, Mr. Grant," she added, "something's very wrong; and my head goes wobbly, and I can't see things when I want to."

A little flat bottle was peeping out of Mrs. Rooney's pocket at that moment, and made me smile.

"It's very hard on you, Mrs. Rooney," I said, "to be so worried; and as I think of it, I'm rather down in the mouth, too. Would you mind obliging me by running over to the Three Blind Mice, and fetching me a bottle of 'unsweetened'?"

"Is there anything in the world I wouldn't do for you?" the widow answered, with an alacrity inspired by anticipated pleasure.

Her smudged sallow face brightened, and she took the proffered coins with greedy fingers. In about five minutes she returned in company with a bottle of gin, already duly opened, two glasses, and a jug of water.

"I never had a young gentleman staying in my house," said Mrs. Rooney, engaged in helping herself to a large measure of the spirit, "as I could feel so much like a mother to as you, Mr. Grant. And as I come to look at you, you do remind me so much of my old man, now dead and gone these ten years" – I gasped a trifle, but she went on unconcernedly – "when my old man was young. You've just got his nose and the bottom part of his chin, though your eyes is different, and your mouth and moustache not a bit like him. And his hair was more fiery like than yours. I suppose that's why I took to you so immediate when you came to me."

I asserted that I felt extremely favoured by the comparison, and soon managed to draw the conversation towards the subject of Mr. Byrne's disappearance.

"Perhaps he has left a letter or some papers," I said, "that might explain his absence."

"Oh, no; he'd have told me," said Mrs. Rooney.

I strongly remonstrated. "It's your duty, Mrs. Rooney, search the place and see if there's anything there that can give a clue to his whereabouts. If anything has happened to the poor man, we must try and find him – that's all. He may have been run over and be in a hospital, and not be able to speak and give his name and address."

I do not know whether my personal persuasion or that of the bottle of "unsweetened" was the more powerful, but Mrs. Rooney at last consented, and unlocked my neighbour's door.

"Yes," I said to myself, as I carefully examined the place and its contents, "that's the sort of room where that infernal box may have been made." There was every machinery there for manufacturing it – tools, vices, soldering materials, jars filled with chemicals, acids by the bottleful. The place was a laboratory and workshop combined. There was a trunk in one corner – a heavy one – but it was locked; and I could see no papers lying about that could afford a clue.

I was anxious not to arouse Mrs. Rooney's suspicions, and preferred to wait before making a thorough search of the place. I was about to leave the room, when I saw, on the little table in the corner, a box of cigarettes. It was a tin box, and as I opened it,

I found it still contained a number of exceedingly fine Egyptian cigarettes.

I looked at it for a second or two; and as I held it in my hand I felt my face grow cold. It was a little box about six inches long, three inches broad, and an inch deep, and from the description I had read in the papers, it was identical with that Satanic one which had contained the poison that killed Lord Senfrey.

I deliberated with myself whether I should take it or not, or whether I had better leave it in its place, to be found as a proof when I wanted it. The box bore no inscription or mark of any kind, but I knew that I could at any time ask Mrs. Rooney for it if I wanted to. I simply opened it, and took out one of the cigarettes, saying casually, "That's just what I wanted. I suppose he won't mind my stealing a cigarette from him, if he comes back. I'd do the same thing for him."

"Take one by all means," said Mrs. Rooney stoutly. "He'd be only too glad, I know, though he can be a bear now and then. But he has always been decent to his neighbours. He was very nice to that poor girl that killed herself, and very kind."

That evening and night I passed in fruitless watching. The next morning I waited in the same way until past noon. Then I strolled out again, taking Sprat with me. I called at my chambers, and then went to Park Lane. I determined to have an interview with Lady Bent, without telling her or allowing her to know what I had discovered.

"My lady isn't very well, and hasn't yet come down," said the footman. "I'll tell her maid, and she'll see you, I've no doubt."

Indeed, Lady Bent's maid came down a few minutes afterwards. "Lady Bent," she said, "will see you in her boudoir. She's poorly this morning, after yesterday's mournful scene."

I was ushered into Lady Bent's room, a dainty and richly decorated little chamber. My lady wore an "old gold" plush dressing-gown, trimmed with rich lace, and her face had an anxious and drawn look, for which the emotions of the previous day might perhaps have proved sufficient warranty. She was smoking a cigarette when I entered, and held out the tips of two fingers.

"You mustn't mind me, Mr. Grey," she said. "I suppose you are shocked at seeing a lady smoke. It's a habit of mine of which I can't break myself, and when I'm a little nervous I fly to it."

I protested that I was not disconcerted in the least, and that I knew that many ladies indulged in a whiff now and then.

I had barely finished my words, however, when, upon the table at my lady's side, I saw a box – the box which contained her cigarettes. It was identically of the same make, shape and size as the one I had seen in Jasper Byrne's room.

Chapter 8

Crowded Hour of Inglorious Life

MY suspicions were well founded, it was quite natural that I might see a box like that in Lady Bent's room. Yet the discovery so surprised me that, for a few heartbeats' space, I gazed at the thing as I might have done at a snake. In nearly the same flash of time, however, I was calm again.

"That's a clever woman," I said to myself. "Those cigarettes were supplied to her by Brodie. She had been smoking them all along; and had she changed the brand or style of boxes it might have attracted attention and aroused suspicion."

Lady Bent evidently noticed that I was ill at ease, for she said, "I do hope that you've brought us good news, Mr. Grey, because I'm so nervous and prostrated this morning."

As she hesitated, I said, "I only came to ask you a question."

She heaved a long sigh. "Go on," she said wearily, as if preparing for torture.

"I want you to give me some information, Lady Bent," I said, "which is of the utmost importance. A banknote – a ten-pound note – has been found in the room in which that girl Orano poisoned herself

"Well!" she ejaculated.

"That note was paid to Lord Bent by his bankers on the second of the present month."

She had been reclining dreamily until then. She rose with parted lips and eyes wide open.

"To Lord Bent?" she asked, with a nervous quiver of the voice.

"Yes," I retorted. "It was issued by the Bank of England to the St. James' Branch of the London and Westminster Bank. They in their turn paid it to Lord Bent." I paused for a second to see the effect of my speech upon her. She had with one hand gripped the satin pillow of her couch, and was crushing it between her fingers. Her teeth were hard set, and she was visibly nerving herself for an onslaught.

"Well! well! well!" she repeated twice or thrice.

"I thought," I went on slowly and measuredly, "I would come to you, Lady Bent, to ask if you knew any person by whose agency that note might have come into Maria Orano's room."

The assault was direct, and she winced beneath it. She looked into my eyes pitifully for a second and gasped.

"I don't quite understand," she whispered hoarsely at last.

"I'll explain myself more fully, Lady Bent," I said; "I came here to you first of all because, to start with, I didn't wish to shock or unnecessarily distress Lord Bent. Secondly, my purpose is – and believe me that in this matter I'm doing my best for everybody concerned – to avoid a public *exposé*. That note was undoubtedly issued to Lord Bent. I repeat my question, and I would ask you, Lady Bent, to weigh it well, and to give me your answer. Do you know anybody to whom, on the second of May, you paid a ten pound note, and who might have given that note to Maria Orano?"

The hunted deer, driven into a hopeless corner of the moors, might look at the pursuing hounds as Lady Bent gazed at me. I noticed the feverish twitching of the fingers and the excited heaving of the bosom, but it was momentarily only. She bit her lip and drew herself up.

"What a question to ask me," she said, with a sickly smile, accompanied by a little peal of laughter, that had no gaiety in it. "How am I to know? I pay my notes to all sorts of people."

I had my own purpose in this interrogatory. It was twofold. It was my business to try to discover whether Lady Bent was a victim or an accomplice of that villain Brodie; and, secondly, if she were an accomplice, I wanted to rouse my Maltese friend from his lethargy of self-confidence. Threatened people and people who think themselves in danger are always more likely to do foolish things and to act unguardedly than persons who think themselves secure, and can weigh their chances with an evenly balanced mind. If Count Brodie thought himself in danger, he would most likely attempt to escape, and thus he would prove a much more easily-hunted quarry.

"Lady Bent," I said, "I'm sorry that you can give me no information. I shall have to ask Lord Bent to trace the note for me. I regret having troubled you, and hope that you'll forgive my intrusion."

I rose and made a movement towards the door. She followed me with her eyes as if she were dazed. Her right hand wandered towards her heart and the other fumbled the air nervously as she hoarsely whispered, "Stay – stay, for a moment, Mr. – Mr. Grey. I'll – I'll see what I can do. I'm flurried and upset. Have pity on a poor woman, and be as patient as you can."

I sat down again.

"Well, my lady, I'm awaiting your answer."

She had bitten her lip so hard that I could see a tiny speck of blood standing upon it. The fingers of one hand had again wandered towards the satin pillow, and were crushing it more hysterically than before. I pitied her for the moment. If she were a victim and not a criminal, she was a miserable by fate persecuted woman indeed. I scanned the face. It was still handsome, but it was hard. Had misfortune or viciousness hardened those features? A woman with such a face might make a terrible struggle for existence, for wealth, for power, for rank, and a woman with such a face might also make, a violent fight against untoward fate and bear its stings and torture with silent courage. I could read nothing there that finally decided me. All of a sudden her fear-hardened features brightened, and nearly a smile spread upon them.

"I can see your drift, Mr. Grey," she said, with a little gasp, and evidently with a fierce struggle to appear unconcerned. "I do remember now, and" – she dropped her voice to a whisper and looked towards the door – "I can also see that it might be wise not to ask Lord Bent about it." She moved a few inches on her seat and approached me more closely. "People's tongues wag dangerously sometimes," she went on, "and a woman like myself cannot afford to set them wagging. As I remember now, I paid two hundred pounds to Count Brodie about that time. It was mostly in ten-pound notes. He had bought some lace for me at a sale at Christie's, and that was part of the money. And you see, Mr. Grey," she added, with another half-hysterical laugh, "people might say all kinds of things if they were told that a note which had passed through my hands was found in that girl's room. What the Count's connection with her can have been—" she drew herself up and her eyes flashed as she spoke – "I cannot fathom, but I suppose it was – charity." A sickly smile parted the lips, and she gasped for breath before she had finished.

I had listened to her and watched her in silence, and even when she ceased I spoke not a word.

"I hope, Mr. Grey," she pleaded, placing her hand upon mine – and I felt it cold and clammy as she did so – "that you will see your way to hush up this business. Of course I could easily explain how I came to pay Count Brodie that money, but I should prefer that Lord Bent knew nothing of it."

I shook my head.

"I cannot see at present how I can avoid informing Lord Bent," I said. "Lady Georgina especially lives in the hope that her dead intended husband's memory should be cleared, and here I've discovered that not Lord Senfrey, but Count Brodie, paid that girl money. I think it is my duty to mention it at the inquest tomorrow."

She rose and stood before me with such terror depicted on her face that I could not help feeling sorry for her.

"Do not!" she gasped, "for Heaven's sake do not! You don't know all and I dare not tell you; but if you knew you would pity me."

"I do know, and I do pity you," I said slowly. "I know the history of Bernard Clankton and Lavinia Meredith."

She threw her arms abroad, and staggered forward for a moment. Then, pressing her hands against her temples, she sank back on the sofa with her face as white as a sheet, and her eyes protruding from their sockets. Her lips had gone ashen-grey, and her whole frame shook as in a palsy. Then she sank down slowly on to her knees and dragged herself towards me, clasping my hands, and crying hoarsely,

"Have pity! Have mercy! Have pity! Have mercy! – for Heaven's sake have mercy!"

I freed my hands from her grip, which I felt tightening nervously, and tried to raise her, but she slipped sideways to the floor, and lay there in a dead faint.

I ran to the bell and rang it, and Lady Bent's maid appeared.

"Your mistress has fainted suddenly," I said. "You'd better see to her and bring her round. When she is well, you can tell her that I will try and see her again tomorrow. If not, when she wants me she can send for me."

I left the house without asking to see either Lord Bent or Lady Georgina. I had sown my seed. I now left it to ripen and to bear fruit.

I returned to James Street that evening. Whether Jasper Byrne were dead or alive, I argued with myself, my little room was the place where, most likely, the first clue would spring up. I had, I thought, most of the threads of the tangled web in my hand, and they all seemed to lead me irresistibly towards Brodie. "Brodie,"

I said to myself, "has had a hand in this, as in the first crime, and patience is the game to play."

On the morrow, Wednesday, the adjourned hearing of the charge against Luigi Orano, and the adjourned inquest upon the body of the dead girl, would both take place. Much might be learnt at either of them, but somehow or other my little room at Mrs. Rooney's had its peculiar magic. It seemed to me like a trap specially prepared in which I might catch the unwary criminal.

That same evening my man Humphrey brought me a letter from Lady Bent. I had left special instructions with Humphrey to bring to me any letter bearing a semblance to the handwriting of Lady Bent, and, to be sure, twilight had barely set in when he came and brought me a missive from her.

"My Dear Mr. Grey" – it ran – *"You know my secret, and you have kept silence so far. This gives me hope that perhaps, after all, you may find it in your heart to have pity on a poor sorely tried woman, and to spare her. If you only knew what a life of trial and unmerited misfortune mine has been, you would have mercy on me. Believe me that I did not know when I gave my hand to Lord Bent that that man was alive. Since then my existence has been one of perpetual torture. I have to show a smiling face to the world, while the terror which surrounds me eats my heart away. I have often thought of ending this life of sham and golden misery, but the one hope that perhaps, after all, some day I might be rid of my millstone has stayed my hand. Come and see me when you can; and in the meantime, for God's sake, keep silent. L. B."*

No reference to the murder of Lord Senfrey! That seemed to be the letter of an innocent woman. Would she have dared to so address me if her hands had been stained with Lord Senfrey's blood, she knowing all the while that I was specially charged to unravel that mystery? Yet the theory of her guilt was not incompatible with the letter she had written, or she might have been an unwilling or an innocent tool in Brodie's hands.

I turned the pros and cons over in my mind, and I said to myself: "A woman who could wear such a mask of deceit to her husband and to the world, hard though her struggle might be, might perhaps – I said to myself, might at a moment of severe temptation consent to the sweeping away of a human creature to leave her path unobstructed."

The next morning came, and there was still no news of Jasper Byrne. Mrs. Rooney's face was more elongated even than before, and her cap as rebellious as ever. She walked about listlessly as I had not seen her, and talked incoherently about her good man, dead these ten years past, and Jasper Byrne, and the girl Orano, and myself – all mixed up in an inextricable jumble.

I was debating within my mind whether or not to go to the hearing of the case against Luigi Orano, when Mrs. Rooney came to me with a face which, whether tearful or happy, none might have told.

"Here's a rum go, Mr. Grant," she said, "and if whether to be pleased or to be savage you was to ask me, I couldn't tell. That there Mr. Byrne has been staying away all this while and him not giving a sign of himself any more'n a mummy in the British Museum. It's enough to make a policeman swear. It's a flying in the face of Providence, it is."

"Oh, you have news of him, then?" I exclaimed.

"Yes," replied Mrs. Rooney, "though what to make of it I don't know any more'n Adam. There's a little red-haired girl downstairs – a cheeky chit – she brought me this note, and asks for the pocketbook out of Mr. Byrne's trunk."

"She wants a pocketbook?" I asked. "Let me have a look at the note, please, Mrs. Rooney."

The good woman handed me the missive. It was written on half a sheet of stained notepaper, and it was worded and spelt as follows:

MISSUS ROONIE,
Plese send me mi pokit-book wats in mi tronk on top 'eres the kei
i'm stain with frens dont you troble about me i'm ol rite I'l come
back next weke.

– JASPER BIRN.

"Have you ever before had a letter from Mr. Byrne?" I asked.

"No," was the answer.

"He isn't a great scholar," I said, not being able to restrain a smile, "and he doesn't know how to spell his own name. What are you going to do?"

"I suppose I must give that girl the pocketbook. He has sent the key."

"Humph!" was my ejaculation. "Do you mind me going with you and having a look at the thing? One never knows – this letter might not come from Mr. Byrne. It might be a forgery."

"You don't mean to say so, Mr. Grant!" cried Mrs. Rooney, aghast. "Do you think as he might have been hocussed and inveigled into some bad place?"

"Quite possible," I said quietly. "I don't say he has been, but such things have happened. Suppose we look at the trunk and pocketbook together."

When the box was opened we found, quite on top of it, a brown leather wallet, smoothed by long wear. I opened it carefully, and saw that it contained in one pocket another case. In one partition there was a ten-pound note. In the others there were some papers.

"There's money in this pocketbook," I said to Mrs. Rooney – "a ten-pound note. I think I'd better take the number of that note before we send it."

"By all means, Mr. Grant," replied Mrs. Rooney. "You're much cleverer than I am, and much more careful; and I'm so glad."

"Very well," I said; "you'd better go down to that girl and ask her to come up. I don't want to be present, but I want to see her; I'd like to get a glimpse of her through the open door, and hear what she has got to say, in case of anything being wrong."

"Right," said Mrs. Rooney, and went downstairs. I flew with the pocketbook to my room, looked at the note, and hastily scribbled the number on a bit of paper. It was C 69939. Then I quickly tore out the second letter-case. It was ornamented by a silver monogram "G. B.," with a coronet on top. It contained several letters.

"That's Count Gyffa Brodie's pocketbook," I said to myself. "He must have lost it, and he's trying to get it back again."

In a flash I also looked over the other papers. One was a letter from Brodie, evidently written to Maria Orano. I took that out also. Others were papers referring to both Brodie and Byrne, but I had not time to rush through them when I already heard footsteps on the lower stairs. I darted back into Byrne's room and threw the pocketbook into the trunk, retaining Count Brodie's case and his letter, which I put into my pocket. The next moment I heard Mrs. Rooney in the next room. I put on my hat, and took my stick, and waited with my ear at my ear trumpet.

"I can't make this out, my dear," Mrs. Rooney was saying. "Where did you say Mr. Byrne was staying?"

"Mr. Byrne 'e's a-styin' with friends," replied a shrill and youthful female voice.

"And why doesn't Mr. Byrne come back himself?" asked Mrs. Rooney.

"You see, 'e can't," the girl answered. "Him an' his friends been on the booze, blind, an' 'e's got the staggers, an' 'e sez, sez 'e, that 'e wants is pockit-book wot's in the trunk."

"And who are Mr. Byrne's friends, if you please?"

"His friends?" retorted the girl. "Gaw along. Wot's it got to do with you?"

"Much, my little dear," was Mrs. Rooney's remonstrance. "I should have liked to have known who Mr. Byrne's friends are."

"You're a downy old woman, you are," exclaimed the girl. "Mr. Byrne's friends – that's Dad an' Leggie."

"And who is your father?" asked Mrs. Rooney, with more complacence and good humour than I had ever given her credit for.

There was a pause, and then the shrill voice pealed out again:

"It ain't none o' your business. Are you goin' to give me the pockit-book, or won't you? – 'cos if you won't, I'm a-goin', that's wot I am. Hookey Walker's my name."

"I'm afraid," suggested Mrs. Rooney, "you've been badly brought up, my dear. But as Mr. Byrne wants the book, there, take it."

The girl replied, "Rumbo!"

I had heard enough, and quietly opened my door, and slipped downstairs, and crossed the road. A minute or two afterwards Mrs. Rooney appeared at the hall door with a girl of about fourteen or fifteen. She was a red-haired little minx of the saucy Cockney gamin type, dressed rather gaudily in a check cotton dress, and a straw hat ornamented by red feathers and a profusion of corn-flowers. No sooner had she gained the street than she ran away at top-speed, and I had to use my limbs nimbly to follow her on the other side. She darted in and out of courts like an eel, and I had to keep pace with her. Luckily she never turned or looked back. When she arrived in Holborn she scrambled on top of an omnibus going to the Bank, and I followed, and sat myself down near the door.

"Oh, she's going to the East End," I said to myself, "to some of the cut-throat dens down by Wapping."

Such, however, was not the case, for at the Holborn Viaduct she got off and rushed down the steps leading to the Farringdon Road, and I kept close to her. Here she evidently thought herself clear of all possible pursuit, for she strolled along blithely, even stopping at one paper shop for fully a minute or two, gawping at the illustrated journals. At Blackfriars Road she took a halfpenny omnibus, which went across the bridge. When she arrived on the southern side of the Thames she turned into Stamford Street, and kept along that thoroughfare until she came to York Road. There she turned sharp up one of the little streets leading to the Belvedere Road, and at the end of it I was just in time to see her dart into a little coffee-shop.

"Oh," I said to myself, "that's the hyena's lair, then."

I crossed the street, and surveyed the house from the opposite side. It was a two-storey building, and at the bottom was one of the ordinary coffee-shops of the poorer class, with the lower part of the window covered with green curtains and the usual list of prices. It looked innocent enough, and as I peered through a crack in the curtain I could see that customers were evidently not plentiful, for the place was empty.

"That doesn't look much like a murderer's den," I argued, "and yet there's something mightily wrong. I shall have to get Morris Angel to rig me out, and pay a visit to this place."

It was only when I again sat in an omnibus taking me over Westminster Bridge that I had time to give a closer glance at the pocketbook and papers I had captured. There was no doubt whatever that the little case had been Count Brodie's property, and by some means or other had come into Jasper Byrne's possession. To regain it Brodie had evidently made use of confederates.

There were altogether four letters in the little case. The first one said:

THE SPORTSMAN'S CLUB,
ALBEMARLE STREET,
May 9th.

MA MIE,
What you ask is impossible. Your brother would discover your
whereabouts. I enclose ten pounds. Try to love me a little more.
Then you will be more patient.
Tout à toi,
GYFFA.

The other three letters ran as follows:

You will kill me in the end. I am sure I am beginning to think that
I would much rather be dead than live like this. Here are the two
hundred pounds. My husband will discover all one of these days,
and then your goose with the golden eggs will be slain. Surely, even
from your point of view, that is not an end to be desired.
L. B.

THE SHERIDAN THEATRE, W.C.
May 8th.

So you did not come to your little Dorothy last night. Shall your
little Dorothy come to you? You naughty man, you knew I wanted
that fifty pounds badly. I fancy I know what kept you. It is that
little Italian. I'll scratch her eyes out – there! Come this evening,
and bring the two ponies.

Yours,
DOROTHY.

202 EATON Square, S.W.
May 12th.

SIR,
For the family's sake I will hear what you have to say.
Yours, etc.,
SENFREY.
MR. GYFFA BRODIE.

It was plain to see that the first letter had been, in some way or other, purloined out of Maria Orano's room probably after her death. The other three were most probably in Brodie's pocketbook when Jasper Byrne obtained possession of it. It mattered little to me at what period or how Byrne got hold of these precious documents, which he had, as it seemed to me, used for the purpose of "squeezing" his companion in crime. The tables had been turned upon him – there was no doubt about that. He was in the hands of Brodie's confederates at that coffee-house, and whether he were dead or alive at that moment, only a visit to the place might have disclosed.

The last short note seemed to me specially important, as it proved that Lord Senfrey had been aware of Lady Bent's bigamy, and had consented to see Count Brodie on the subject. Had that terrible knowledge proved fatal to him? I thought, yes, certainly.

I stopped at Craven Street on the road, and there I had time to compare the number of the note in Jasper Byrne's pocketbook, which I had scribbled down, with the number of the note I had found in Maria Orano's flowerpot. One was C 69935, and the other C 69939. Both had evidently been issued the same day and to the same person. Both had come through Lord Bent and Lady Bent to Count Brodie. The net was closing, I thought. One dash and the solution of the mystery might be in my hands. If that coffee-house in the Belvedere Road was the den of cut-throats which I took it to be, it might be dangerous for a man to venture within single-handed. I thought it was worthwhile risking. I was young and strong. I could fight many men of my own weight, and most men below it. I had a good friend in my pocket in the shape of a six-shooter. If "Dad" and "Leggie" were the scoundrels which Count Brodie's confidence warranted them, they would kill me without remorse if they discovered my game. "Well," I thought, "a man can die but once, so here goes."

Chapter 9

A Nice Little Crib

I HAD to prepare perhaps, for prolonged absence. I had left Sprat at James' Street, and therefore rushed back to Mrs. Rooney's. The good woman was in a state of great pother.

"I don't know as I've been doing right, Mr. Grant," she said, "allowing that red-haired hussy to take that thing away with a ten-pound note in it, and me not taking a receipt, and not having a bit of paper to show for it."

"It doesn't matter, Mrs. Rooney," I said. "That piece of paper and the key which the girl brought will always exonerate you."

A knock at the door disturbed us at that moment, and I went upstairs to my room. I looked about my drawers to see what odds and ends I could pick out that would go to make up the belongings of a sailor. I found but little that was of any use. While I was thus engaged Mrs. Rooney entered.

"There's a poor gentleman downstairs – a foreigner gentleman," she said, "the brother of that poor girl that killed herself in your room."

"Oh, they've let him out, then?"

"Yes," she replied; "they've let him out, and he's asking, with tears in his eyes, to be allowed to come and look at this room; but, of course, I wouldn't say 'yes' till I'd asked you."

The police had evidently discovered no evidence to connect Orano with the murder of Lord Senfrey.

"By all means let him come up," I said, being glad to take advantage of this visit to make the young man's acquaintance.

I held out my hand to him as he stood in the doorway a minute or so afterwards, but he simply bowed with a cavalier-like courtesy. He was still dressed in a black velvet coat. His olive complexion had become a nearly greenish-yellow. His dark eyes and black moustache and hair, together with the gleaming white teeth, gave his face a look of peculiar ferocity which, perhaps, it did not deserve. He stood still on the threshold for a score of seconds, and then entered the room and gazed slowly right and left. His chest heaved, and I could see his white teeth close and his fists clench. At last he made a step toward the bed, and, reaching out a wildly fumbling hand, he touched the coverlet. Then, turning towards me, he said, "Here she die?"

There was a pause of excessive silence. He slowly put both hands on the coverlet of my bed, allowing his head to droop on to them. Then he burst out sobbing, as I have never before heard a man, muttering words of endearment in Italian. After a while he rose slowly and wiped his eyes.

"Excuse, sir. I could not help, I loved her so. My only sister." Then he gnashed his teeth again and shook his fist. "Oh, if te scoundrel were alive who kill her! T'ey say I kill him. I not kill him. I wish I kill him; but I not kill him."

I stepped forward.

"I'm very sorry for you," I said. "I can feel what a loss it must be to you."

He gripped my hand quickly and fervidly.

"T'ank you," he repeated twice or thrice. Then, looking at me with a long and searching face, he said, "You sleep on t'is bed where she die?" His head nodded involuntarily as he spoke, and he breathed heavily. "She my only sister," he said, in his quaint, musical Italian accent. "When my mother die I promise take care of her. She die. Ah ogni cosa è rimedio fuora ch'alla morte.

No hope now. I not more can keep promise." He approached me again, and gripped my hand. "You let me come here," he said. "You let me stay one minute, two minute, five minute in your room. They bury her. I know not where."

"Of course you can come whenever you wish," I rejoined. "I shall be very pleased if what I can do will afford some solace to you. There's only one thing I want to say to you. It is your impression that Lord Senfrey's conduct was the cause of your sister's suicide. Don't be sure of that. That your sister was betrayed is beyond question of a doubt. But my idea is that the man who betrayed her lives at this very moment."

He clutched me by the shoulder, and, holding me at arm's length, looked straight into my eyes.

"Show him to me!" he cried fiercely. "Let me see t'e man. Let me look his eyes, and—" His limbs quivered, his teeth were hard set, and speech seemed to be arrested, in his fury. "I have been in prison," he went on. "I have suffer shame – degradation – and my sister dead. I not able go see her buried. Who is it?"

"That I can't tell; at present, at any rate," I rejoined. "But if you come to me again, perhaps something more may be discovered." He glanced at me curiously.

"What your name?" he asked. "What your business?"

"My name is George Grant," I said, "and I'm a draughtsman."

A sickly smile gleamed on his face, seemingly in spite of him.

"Oh!" he said, "you artist? Sorry for you. Artist poor business. But I come again, and if you know anyt'ing you tell me. Now, tank you, and goodbye."

He was gone before either Mrs. Rooney or myself could say a word. We both stood there silently, while we heard his slow and measured steps on the stairs, until the hall door latch clicked, and we knew him to be outside.

"Poor gentleman!" said Mrs. Rooney. "He looked so much like her; only she was prettier in her foreign fashion."

"There's a man," I said to myself, "who would kill Gyffa Brodie as he would a snake, if he were aware of the villain's connection with his sister. He would rid my Lady Bent of her millstone, and hold his life as nothing in the task. The police, I think, must have a clear clue in another direction, else they would not have consented to allow his going free."

I found that, after all, it was useless to take any of the odds and ends I had brought with me; therefore, taking Sprat under my arm, I went downstairs and told Mrs. Rooney that I had to go away on business, and I did not know how long my business might be. It might be a day, or a week, or two weeks, I said. If I should have to be away longer than that, I would send my rent to her all the same.

"And please don't mention it, sir," the old woman retorted. "Don't think of it, sir. Whenever you come back is plenty of time, though money is scarce nowadays, when one's a widow, with her old man dead these ten years."

"I quite understand that," I interrupted; "and you shall not have to wait for me, at any rate."

From Holborn I went straight to Shaftesbury Avenue, to the emporium where Morris Angel provides theatres large and small, and non-theatrical people into the bargain, with outfits and costumes of all kinds, from a knight's suit of armour to a rag picker's dress. I selected a well-worn outfit which had belonged to a seafaring man. Then I went to my chambers in Northumberland Avenue, and having once more consigned Sprat to the care of my man Humphrey, I dressed myself in the newly purchased habiliments. I was well aware that actual disguise for my face would be impossible, as I might have to stay away for some time and to bear close scrutiny. But a very slight coating of Vandyke brown rubbed into the skin until the dry colour clung to it, and could no longer be removed with a rag, gave to my face a very much darker aspect. I put a small packet of the dry colour into my pocket. Then I dishevelled my hair, and brushed my moustache upward. Nobody who has not tried a similar procedure can be aware to what a degree a man's appearance is changed by such a process. At Morris Angel's I had purchased an old carpet bag, with a few worn-out sailors' shirts, trousers, neck handkerchiefs, etc. To these I added an old pair of boots, an old coat, socks, a piece of soap, a comb and a few other trifles; and thus equipped, I set out for Belvedere Road.

I entered the coffee shop boldly, and found a tall, wirily built man in the early fifties, with iron grey beard and hair, and a sinister face, with a skin like drawn parchment, shirt-sleeved and white-aproned, pouring out a couple of cups of tea at the farther end of the shop. That was evidently "Dad," I thought. He walked up to me briskly and surlily, as I seated myself in one of the boxes.

"Wot for you?" he asked.

"I want a cup of tea," I answered, "and a rasher of bacon and some bread and butter."

"Oh, you do," he retorted. "You'll have to wait, then. There's other customers afore you."

With that he returned to the rear, and left me to look about.

Two navvies were seated in the opposite box, big, broad-shouldered specimens of their class, smothered from head to foot in mason's dust, their boots looking as if they had walked on nothing but red mud for years. They were clothed in the usual corduroys, rubbed white by wear, the trousers tied by bits of string below the knees.

"I don't approve of dynamite," one of them was holding forth, crashing down his fist upon the table, which seemed in danger of demolition; "but I approves of hitting 'em over the head with sticks, I does; and I approves of chucking 'em in the river, I does; and I approves of brickbats, I does – big ones. I approves of anything that's fair and English, I does. None of your furrin dodges for me. Rights of labour!" he snorted. "There ain't no rights of labour. It's all wrongs of labour. I tell you, mate, there won't be no rights of labour until every man gets a bob an hour whether he can do anything or can't; and when we've got that, mate," he shouted, "then we'll want more, and let them look out as don't give it."

The fist again came down with an awful bang, and he cast a ferocious glance at me.

"What a nuisance that man is," I said to myself. "He will prevent me from having a quiet talk with that parchment-faced landlord there."

As I looked again, I thought I had seen the burly socialist's face before. To be sure, as I gazed more closely, I recognised it as that of the bearded policeman in plain clothes who had shadowed me from Mrs. Garrison's window opposite; and my respect for the Metropolitan Criminal Investigation Department correspondingly increased.

I sat open-mouthed for a few moments' space, my surprise was so great. Here I had barely spent two or three hours, and they were in the place before me. That was not bad. The man's disguise was wonderful. He looked every inch the real thing, and acted it as well.

"That's all very well, mate," responded the second man, quite as much up to his *rôle* as his companion. "But wot's them to do that's got no work to do? How is them to be paid? Is they to have a bob an hour? That's wot I wants to know; for wot's the good of a bob an hour to a man when he ain't got no bob an hour to get?"

The first policeman in disguise scratched his head at this. His mate's social economy was evidently overpowering.

"Well," he rejoined, "if you was to ax me, and if them there County-Councillors, that ain't no more good than a three-legged sheep, barring the bleating – if they was to ax me, I'd tell 'em: they wot's got no work and can take their livin' oath afore a judge and jury as they can't get none, them, I say, is to have a bob an hour as well." Hereupon he straightened himself, and looked defiantly at the landlord, who approached with the tray and tea things. Yes," he said, "I'd give every man, as is a man, a bob an hour."

The landlord, having placed the cup of tea, squared his elbows.

"And who's to pay for it, please?" he asked. "I'm a 'ouse 'older and a rate-payer, and I ain't goin' to pay for no hulkin' loafers doin' nothing and robbin' the parish."

The burly man snapped his fingers at the landlord's nose. "That's all you know," he said. "If them as brought you up had taught you readin' and writin' and philosophicks, they'd a told you as the ratepayers ain't got nothink to do with them there questions. It's himperial it is, and not paroakal."

Hereupon the landlord opened his eyes.

"And who's to pay for it, then?" he repeated.

"The swells. Them as has millions, when I've got only three bob and a kick. Them as eats rabbit and salt pork, when he got to be satisfied with a two-eyed steak. Them as drink beer by the quarts and get boozed when they likes, when I've got to wash myself out with your skilly rot."

The parchment-faced man bridled up at this. Don't you go slanderin' my tea," he said. "It's been good enough for your betters, and is good enough for the likes of you."

I thought it was time to interpose.

"Stop that jaw," I cried, in my gruffest tones. "I want my tea. Rot your politics. We're here to eat and drink, not to spout."

Hereupon the burly man rose and crossed over to me. He stood at the end of the table of my box, resting on his hands and bent forward.

"And wot's it got to do with you?" he asked roughly.

The coffee-house keeper had walked to the further end of the room, and the broad back was squared against him, so that he could not see the burly man's face. The detective looked cautiously over his shoulder, and then winked meaningly. I took no notice of the sign.

"It has got a lot to do with me," I retorted. "I'm hungry, and I want my grub. You stay in your box and feed, and let me have my tea."

"O.K., Cocky Wax," rejoined the burly man. "You've swallered the pepper box and got thirsty, you have. Gaw away, and try to be a little more politer when next a gennelman tries to teach you wot you don't know."

"Here! here, you two!" shouted the landlord. "Don't you go quarrelling in my place, else I chucks you both."

"Come on," shouted the big man, "I'm a waitin' to be chucked."

The landlord's ardour was apparently not thorough-paced, for he made no movement, but simply exclaimed: "Well, then, behave yourselves. I don't want the row in my place."

With this he disappeared behind the little door, which led, most probably, to his kitchen. I looked round the place, and quickly espied another door at the farther end of the room, and, without further ado, walked up to it and opened it. It led into a long and nearly dark passage. I had barely advanced half a dozen steps when I became aware of a peculiar acrid and medicinal odour, which lay heavy upon the air and gripped my lungs pungently. But before I had time to further investigate it, the door behind me was opened again, and the shrill voice of the little red-haired minx was heard there. "Eh, you there! I like your cheek. Come aht o' that!"

I pretended not to hear, and fumbled on, when the little minx ran after me and caught hold of me by the shirt sleeves.

"Where are you goin'?" she said. "You ayn't got no bisniss 'ere."

The parchment-faced man appeared at the opposite end at that moment, and I deemed a prolonged investigation unwise.

"'Ere – you! What are you walking about there for? Out you come!"

I re-entered the room slowly.

"What a fuss you're making," I said quietly. "One would think you'd got something to hide there. I was doing no harm."

"Harm or no harm," snarled the shopkeeper, "you ain't got no business in there. Perhaps you'd like to buy the shop and 'ouse and all for your fourpence ha'penny?"

"I don't want your house and shop," I answered. "I want my tea, and I want to know if I can have a bed here."

"No," was the gruff reply. "We don't let no beds 'ere."

The burly man in the opposite box sped a knowing wink towards me, which elicited no reply. While I was eating the food placed before me I tried to think from what chemical proceeded the odour which had reached me in the passage.

"I've hit it," I said to myself. "It's opium, opium; but not opium alone! They're poisoning him out there somewhere."

The premises behind and above the coffee-shop being barred to me, further stay for the moment was useless. I left the shop, and looked right and left for possible lodgings. Most people in that road let rooms; and as luck would have it, the very next house had a little bill over the door – "A bedroom to let." I knocked, and found a slatternly middle-aged Irish woman, who informed me that the bedroom was at the back of the house on the first floor. I was shown into it, and found it a pokey little place, with only a small iron bedstead, a washstand, a rickety chest of drawers and a chair in it. I paid the rent demanded for it, four and sixpence a week, in advance, and was immediately installed.

"I haven't gained much," I said, as I looked out into the courtyard.

Opposite me loomed a dead, whitewashed wall some eighteen feet high. As far as I could see, it formed the back of an out-building which led from the coffee shop towards a shed at the back of the yard. I could see very little of the last erection except the roof, which was flat and of lead, and seemed to have a ramshackle skylight in it. What little I could discover of the construction of the shed seemed to be tumble-down brick, and it had the appearance of being, or having been, used as a workshop. It might have been a washhouse.

"That's the place," I said to myself, "from which that medicinal smell came."

I looked further. A great stack of timber loomed just beyond the shed, thus securing absolute privacy on that side. At the back there was more timber. The courtyard of the house in which I lived was connected with the bare wall opposite me by one a little lower, some fourteen feet high, perhaps. I surveyed the field of my possible operations. There was no way of getting into the next yard or into the shed except by climbing out of my window on to the low wall at the back, a proceeding fraught with difficulty. Then, by going along the top of the wall, I might easily swing myself on to the roof of the shed. But, of course, all that was impossible in daylight. I had to bide my time until darkness came to my aid.

I arranged my things, and then went out, walking round the block in which my newly found lodgings stood, for the purpose of gaining a general idea of its position and the avenues of escape, in case egress, through the front were barred. A huge factory blocked the way on the south, and on the east other houses, fully tenanted, lined the sides of the street. On the west only exit seemed possible. The big timber yard afforded a ready place of refuge.

It had been murky all along, and now a fine drizzle set in. I returned to my room. As it grew darker, the drizzle changed to a steady rain, which, after half an hour or so, became a regular downpour. The water splashed on the roof of the shed opposite to me with quite a pretty roar. The sky was black, and the darkness became dense.

"Now's my time," I said to myself.

I took off my coat and waistcoat, and put on an old pair of trousers. Then I threw off my boots, so as to be able to move noiselessly. I next opened my window and looked out. Nothing but the pitchy pall of the night. No light gleamed in any of the windows close by. Whether the people in the coffee shop were awake or not, nobody might have told. Some distance farther on two or three pale yellow blotches stood out in the murky space; but beyond that nothing. I pushed my head out of the window, and, firmly gripping the wooden frame, I allowed myself to slide down outside, kicking the air for a foothold on the low wall at the end of the yard. After an effort, during which my grip nearly gave way and my fingers became numbed, I managed to put my foot on the place.

Then I caught hold of the water-pipe at the end of the house, and, thus steadying myself, knelt down on the coping.

A storm broke loose at that moment. The lightning flashed and the thunder rattled. There were moments when the lightning throbbed with a white heat on the heavens, lighting up the scene all round, and I was afraid of being noticed. I crawled along on my stomach, and, after a little space, reached the top of the shed opposite. There I lay down and listened between the crashes, but heard nothing. Then I dragged myself along again, pausing and lying flat at times. The rain splashed and hissed and sputtered, and the roar of the thunder altogether drowned the noise of my guarded movements,

I reached the skylight and looked down. All was black as pitch below – nothing but a great inky void. I had my ear close to the glass, but not a sound reached me for a long while. At last, even in the midst of the bellowing thunder, a low moan faintly rose to my ear, and a voice called a name which I did not understand.

I had been lying there in the furious rain for half an hour, perhaps, and my limbs had become stiff and numb, when, all of a sudden, a light shot into the room below, and as I peered down with burning eyes, I could see that it came from a candle held by the parchment-faced man.

"Wot d'ye want now?" he shouted gruffly to someone below. I searched the space below by the fitful gleam. The coffee shop keeper had approached a low couch – a truckle bed most likely – on which lay a man. The light fell on his features at that moment and lit them up with a curious Rembrandtesque glow, and I could see them ghastly ashen. It was Jasper Byrne; but Jasper Byrne wan and wasted, his face like a death mask. I could see the shaking hand, which he tried to raise, and the eyes which glared uncannily as the light was reflected on them. The thunder had ceased just then, and the splashing rain was the only noise audible above, except now and then the low whish and wail of the wind. I lay still as a corpse, and listened with my heart in my ears.

"I want to go away," Byrne gasped hoarsely. "You're killing me. I know you are. You're not giving me anything to make me well again. I am dying."

"Rubbish!" retorted the man. "You hold your row, or it'll be the wuss for you. The Count's 'ere."

Another figure entered the place at that moment. I recognised it immediately as Brodie, in spite of the big ulster with upturned collar and the slouch hat which he wore. The Maltese immediately stepped to the little bed.

"You have deceived me!" he cried in French. "My case was not in that wallet. Tell me where you have put it, or I will strangle you."

The poor man shrank back on his couch.

"Oh, no!" he cried. "I told you right. I told you the truth. It was in my pocketbook."

"It was not," retorted Brodie. "You stole it, and you have hidden it, you villain. You want to keep it still; but I will drag it from you. So you thought you could play your game with me!"

He rushed at the reclining figure, and shook it roughly. I will shake the life out of you, if you do not tell me the truth."

Byrne raised a nervously fumbling hand to guard against his cowardly aggressor, and I could hear the creaking of the little couch under Brodie's violence. Then the moans ceased, and all was silent for a moment.

"He's told a lie, then?" asked the coffee-house keeper.

"Yes," replied Brodie. "My case was not in that wallet. The wretch stole it to keep a hold over me, and we'll have to get it back somehow."

A moment afterwards all was darkness again below.

I had heard enough, and crawling carefully back, reached my room.

I looked and felt much more like a drowned rat than a man, but I thought myself well repaid.

Chapter 10

Untwisting All the Chain

WHEN I restored my sluggard circulation by rubbing myself with a dry towel, I deliberated with myself about the best course of action. Jasper Byrne was being poisoned by these wretches, there was no doubt about that. If he remained in their clutches for another night and another day, there would probably be an end of him. Of course it was quite within my power to give information to the police and then have him dragged out of this murderer's den, but as I came to turn it over in my mind, I decided to undertake the task myself. Jasper Byrne would prove a most useful person; if I gained his confidence, my path might be cleared of many difficulties.

It was not an easy task, however. As far as I could judge, he was extremely weak, and would have to be lifted bodily to the roof of the shed, and then carried along that narrow wall and raised through the window of my room. An unguarded or untoward movement might result in my breaking my neck. In addition to that, the task would have to be undertaken when all was absolutely quiet, and it was only possible if Jasper Byrne were left unguarded in his shed.

The thunders had ceased to growl, but the rain swished on as furiously as before. It was a regular deluge. The night was still dark as pitch. Before twilight had set in, I had noticed that my landlady had left her clothes-lines stretched from wall to wall in the courtyard, and I made up my mind to use these in my work.

I waited until Big Ben struck two. All was still as death. Not a sound anywhere. The rain had abated its fury, and was a steady, penetrating drizzle. The first thing I had to do was to reach the yard. That was not difficult. I got out of my window as before, climbed down the waterpipe in the corner, and immediately secured something like forty yards of stout clothes-line. These I coiled together and slung them across my shoulder. Then I climbed back to the partition wall in the manner I had come, and soon was on top of the shed opposite.

I looked about me. No light anywhere. I crawled on hands and knees along the roof of the outhouse, which reached from the shed to the coffee-shop building itself. There I lay down and listened. No sound, no breath. I peered into the darkness in every direction, but no light, no sound of life anywhere.

I returned, still on my hands and knees, to the roof of the shed, and found the skylight. I tried to lift it, but failed. I felt with groping fingers for the edges of the frame. The putty, though soaked on top by the rain, was dry as dust underneath, and crumbled away under my touch. I took out my clasp-knife, and, as quickly as I could, removed the putty from one frame. Then I inserted my knife to lift the sheet of glass; but, as bad luck would have it, the glass was probably cracked, for a piece escaped me and fell with a little crash to the floor below.

I lay quite still and listened. I could see nothing in the shed, but I could hear a movement and a little cry of surprise. After that, a silence as of death. Jasper Byrne was evidently alone, and nobody had heard me.

Undaunted, I went on and ripped the putty from another sheet of glass. There I was more successful, and the aperture was larger. I had barely succeeded when I heard a movement below and a faint cry. Again I listened. The movements continued, but no other living presence made itself known. I lay down on the roof and called "Mr. Byrne!" and a scarcely audible "Who is it? For God's sake, who is it – who calls me?" was the reply.

"I'm a friend," I said. "Keep quiet and listen. I'm here to rescue you."

There was a slight pause, during which I thought I could hear my heartbeat against my ribs. Then came the answer:

"Thank God! Thank God!"

"Don't be frightened at anything I may do," I said. "Lie quiet, and give no sign."

I felt with my hand along the edge of the aperture which I had made, and managed to reach the latch, which, on the inside, held the skylight fastened down. It was rusted into the catch, and it was only by a desperate effort that I succeeded in loosening it. After that it was easy to raise the skylight and give an opening large enough to admit three men.

The next question was how to descend. I could see nothing in the pitchy darkness, but the distance from the roof to the floor could not be more than about twelve feet. I uncoiled a portion of my clothes-line and fastened about twenty yards of it to the solid iron staple which formed the catch of the skylight latch, and slid along it in a heartbeat's space. Luckily for myself, I had brought my fuse box, and when I had reached the bottom I struck a match.

A swift glance around the place showed me a corner where my way up would be easier, on each side of the skylight great beams ran right and left from the wall to the roof. Even if the staple gave way, I could reach the roof.

I struck another match and peered into Jasper Byrne's face. I had never seen such a ghastly grey face before. The lips were blue; his whole frame shook as in an ague. He would have to be carried like a child. He looked at me curiously for a second.

"Why, you're the man in the next room to me at Mrs. Rooney's!" he gasped hoarsely.

"I am," I replied. "I discovered that you were in danger of being murdered, and I'll take you back to Mrs. Rooney's tonight, but for Heaven's sake don't whisper even. You are not strong enough to move, I suppose?"

He raised himself painfully, and then I saw that he was dressed in his trousers and a check cotton shirt.

"Have you your boots here?" I asked.

He shook his head.

"No coat?"

Again he shook his head

"Well, we'll have to do without them," I said. "Now, do exactly what I tell you. You must let me arrange you in such a way that I can carry you, as I would a baby, on my back."

So saying, I lifted him up, and seated him on the bed with his back to the wall. Then I knelt down in front of him with my back towards him.

"Now," I said, "fling your arms around my neck, and try to clutch me with your legs."

He made a feeble effort, and at last succeeded. In the meantime I held some ten or twelve yards of clothes-line between my teeth. I threw a double coil of the rope behind my back, catching him underneath the arms. This I fastened across my chest; then by dint of much fumbling I pushed the ends between my legs and caught his legs. These I tied as best I could. Movement was of course impeded this way, but if the poor fellow's strength failed, it might save me and him from breaking our necks."

"Now," I said, "hold on to my neck with all your strength. Your life and mine may depend upon it."

I could feel his bony fingers closing with the grip of despair across my breast, and his nails digging into my flesh. As I raised myself, I found that, after all, he seemed to be no great drag. I pushed the bed against the wall where I could clutch the beam, and swung myself up with it. Then I caught the rope which was hanging loosely from the staple, and although the iron creaked and the rope strained in imminent danger of snapping,

I managed to swing myself up to the skylight and drag myself through it, with Byrne clinging desperately to my back. Once out, I unfastened the rope and coiled it around Byrne's body and mine, to give added security. I crawled back on my hands and knees along the narrow coping of the partition wall; but the severest trial came when I attempted to reach my own window. Here I nearly missed my footing, and only by a hair's breadth escaped tumbling headlong down into the paved yard. I never thought that I should be able to lift the dead weight on my back into the window. But at last I managed it, and Byrne and myself were in security in my room.

Fortunately for both of us, the rain had ceased. I was as soaked as before, but Jasper Byrne's clothing was dry, except where it had come into contact with mine. There was no time to be lost. Therefore I dressed Byrne in my coat, and fitted him with a pair of old shoes I had brought with me. An old soft felt hat of mine completed his attire.

That being done, I decided not to lose a second, but taking him in my arms, I carried him downstairs. The hall door was locked and bolted, and the noise which I had to make in unbolting it brought somebody to the top landing, and a woman's voice called out shrilly,

"Who's that down there? What are you doing?"

"It's only I," I replied. "I've got to go to my work."

"Do you work at three o'clock in the morning?" shouted the voice. "Yes, at three o'clock in the morning," I replied; but by that time, having drawn all the bolts, I went out and slammed the door behind me. It was a matter of indifference to me what my good landlady might care to do afterwards.

All was quiet in the street. Not a sound. I walked along Belvedere Road, carrying Jasper Byrne. He was not very heavy, but he felt more like an inanimate object in my arms than a live man. At the corner of the Westminster Road the steady tramp of a policeman came towards me, and after proceeding a score of paces I saw the constable. He flashed his bull's-eye at me, and said,

"Where are you going to with that man?"

"It's a poor pal of mine," I replied, "that is dying, I think; and I'm going to see if I can get him in a hospital."

The round disk of light was full on Jasper Byrne's face for some ten or twelve seconds.

"He does look bad," said the policeman softly. "He looks as if a hospital wouldn't be able to do much good to him. But they won't take him in at this time of night."

"I think they will," I replied. "They'll take him in at the Free Hospital in Gray's Inn Road, if I can only find a cab."

The policeman's bull's-eye flashed into my face and travelled over me.

"Go on then," he said; "and I hope you'll succeed. Stop for a moment," he added; "you might give me your name."

"George Grant," I rejoined, "212, Belvedere Road."

The policeman flashed his light at me again, and jotted down the name and address in his book.

"Run on," he said. "The sooner a doctor sees your pal the better it will be for him."

On Westminster Bridge I met a crawling cab, and the offer of three shillings was sufficient to ensure the driver's best services.

I shall not soon forget Mrs. Rooney's face when, after ringing and knocking as if I had intended to tear the house down, she opened the door. The poor woman fairly screamed.

"Is it Mr. Byrne?" she said, "or is it his ghost? Good heavens! He isn't dead, is he?"

"No, he isn't dead," I said, "but he may die, unless we do something immediately to bring him round."

"Poor Mr. Byrne!" blubbered Mrs. Rooney, when I had carried the man upstairs and laid him on his bed. "What have they been doing to him, the villains? And you, Mr. Grant; what have you been and done to yourself, looking for all the world as if you'd been trying to sweep the streets? And look at your clothes."

"Run, Mrs. Rooney!" I interrupted; "make a cup of coffee as strong and as hot as you can, and fly for your life."

She looked at me for a second in amazed enquiry.

"Run!" I went on. "This man's life may depend on what you do."

I lighted a candle. Byrne lay upon his bed like a log. But for a barely perceptible breathing he might have been dead. His face was grey, his lips nearly green, his eyes closed. That he was suffering from some narcotic poisoning was beyond question; but to my mind he was not suffering from narcotic poisoning alone. The feebleness of the pulse, the absence of perspiration, and, when I tried it, the swift effect of the light of my candle upon the pupils proved to me that there was a preponderance most likely of another venom, probably a metallic one."

Mrs. Rooney soon came, with a steaming cup of coffee in her hand. I administered a spoonful of it at a time, as best I could, to the patient, and though it had but little visible effect upon him, I knew, from the slightly stronger breathing and from the weak effort to rouse himself, that I had done right.

I did not care to bear the responsibility of this man's life or death, especially as I was perfectly in the dark about what had happened to him. Therefore I sent Mrs. Rooney for her doctor, who arrived about half an hour afterwards in hot haste, not at all over-pleased at being called out of his bed at that time of the morning. He was a grumpy man, prematurely bald, with stubby, reddish-brown whiskers. When he saw Byrne he shook his head.

"The man has been taking opium," he said; "that's as plain as daylight. A filthy habit, and he deserves all he has got."

"But what are we to do, doctor?" I asked.

"Do?" he growled. "I wish I'd known it was a case like this when I was called out of my bed just as I got a wink of sleep, after being up half the night with an accident case. Do? No use trying a stomach pump with him; he's soaked with it. Might try an emetic. Put cold wet towels on his head and chest. Try and keep him awake. If you haven't any compound camphor liniment in the house, put a poultice of mustard and cayenne pepper on him, and as soon as it's daylight, you can send for some sal volatile and let him breathe that."

"I've given him a portion of a cup of coffee," I said. "I suppose I wasn't doing wrong?"

"Not at all," he said gruffly. "Punch him – jump on him – but keep him awake. Good morning."

"What's that nice gentleman's name?" I asked Mrs. Rooney, when the surgeon had left the room.

"That's Doctor Benderley," she said. "He's not very nice as a rule, but I never knew him to be a boor like that."

It struck me very forcibly that Doctor Benderley carried on his shoulders a very grave responsibility, and that if Jasper Byrne died, serious questions might be put to the worthy doctor as to whether or nay he had given the sufficient attention. The treatment which he prescribed I knew to be quite correct in the case of poisoning by opium, but I feared, and, indeed, thought I knew, that opium was not the only dangerous substance with which Byrne had been drugged.

Mrs. Rooney and myself spent the next few hours in carrying out Doctor Benderley's instructions, slightly varied in such a manner as my common sense and general medical knowledge warranted. It was nearly nine o'clock before I felt a little easier. The pulse had become stronger, the breathing more free, and the movements less painful and palsied.

I had barely time to wash, and dress myself in decent clothing, when Mrs. Rooney came to me and said, "If you please Mr. Grant, there's a gentleman downstairs wants to see you. He won't give me his name, but he says that he knows Mr. George Grey, and that that will be introduction enough for you."

I asked Mrs. Rooney to show the gentleman into my room.

My visitor proved to be Mr. Inspector Warder, of the Criminal Investigation Department of the Metropolitan Police, whom I knew to be charged with the unravelling of the Senfrey mystery. He looked at me with a smile, and held out his hand.

"My name's Warder," he said. "I suppose you know me?"

"Yes," I replied, "I do know you."

"You'll forgive me if I take a seat," he added, without further ado, and suited the action to the word. "So you are 'G. G.'?" he continued.

"Yes," I replied, closing the door. "I am G. G; but that is no reason why all the world should know it."

"Right!" he answered. "You're quite right. I'll moderate the exuberance of my voice. You've got this Senfrey case in hand for the family?"

"Yes," I replied, "I have."

"Well," he went on, patting his knees and looking down at the floor as if he were trying to find a sixpence which somebody had lost there, "I've also got the Senfrey case in hand; and it strikes me that whatever you find out, when it comes to the real thing and you want the man – he looked at me straight at that word – "or the woman who did it locked up, you'll have to come to one of us to do it."

"Quite right," I said; "absolutely right. I should come to one of you to do it."

"Well," he continued, tapping his knee with his open palm, "I'll be straightforward and above board with you. I've been having you shadowed, and I've kept up an even running with you until last night. Last night, the man who was shadowing you watched that coffee house in the Belvedere Road, and stayed until the shop was closed at midnight, and for an hour after that; but as it was pouring cats and dogs, he thought that nobody would come out in that filthy weather, and went home to change his clothes. He went back at half-past three in the morning and stayed, but the shop remained shut, and when we broke into it about an hour and a half ago, we found that the two men who lived there and the girl had hooked it – got out by way of the timber-yard at the back. And when we enquired further into the business, we found that you'd got out of your place about three in the morning, and my men opposite here tell me that you and another man came home shortly after that."

"All that's quite true, Mr. Warder," I said.

He held out his hand again.

"Let's be pals," he said. "I'm Warder and you're G. G. I'm not one of those who want all the fat for themselves and leave all the gristle and work to others. I've seen enough of you to know that you're a deep one. But, as I said before, in any case when it comes to the real business, you'll have to come to one of us."

"Quite right again," I said.

"What I want to propose to you is this. Let that 'one of us' be me. You live in this house and you can get on faster than I can. I don't want to take your credit away from you, and we both are working for the same end. If you promise that when you want an arrest made I shall make it, I won't work against you. Is it a bargain?"

"It is," I said; "and the best proof that I can give you that I'm straightforward is this. – Come with me."

I went to the next room and showed him Byrne.

"So that's the man," he said, when we were in my room again, "whom you brought here? Did you find him in that hole?"

"I did."

"And you got him out through the skylight?" he exclaimed, looking at me in wonderment. "It must have been a stiff job."

"It was a stiff job," I said. "They've been trying to murder him, and I promise you, Warder, that though these two men and the girl have got away, you shall lay your hand upon the shoulder of the principal villain before a fortnight's over. Let us give him rope enough – that's all."

"All right," he answered; and shaking my hand again, said, "Goodbye, for the present," and went away.

As I looked out of my window, I could see him enter Mrs. Garrison's house opposite. There were three men instead of two at that moment walking up and down in the street below. A cab was waiting by the kerb a little farther down the roadway, and I had little doubt that Mrs. Garrison's house held quite a force.

Shortly after that I went out and telegraphed Humphrey, who brought me a fresh supply of linen, and also Sprat. I felt that the little doggie was my mascot, and did not care to be without him.

Byrne got better with astonishing rapidity, That same evening I could see that he was out of immediate danger. I passed the next three or four days in bestowing all my attention upon my neighbour. I carefully avoided all reference to his rescue or to his connection with Count Brodie, and he seemed to be afraid of questioning me. Now and then he would look at me with a gaze of puzzled enquiry, and twice or thrice he said, "You've been very good to me, Mr. Grant. You risked your life for me," evidently endeavouring to elicit an expression from me or a question; but I always said, "Don't mention it. All you've got to do is to get better."

Inspector Warder called every morning, and on the Sunday morning, after he had left me, Mrs. Rooney came running up to me in hot haste.

"Do you know who that gentleman is who come to see you every day?"

"Of course I do," I answered.

"You don't mean to say so!" she exclaimed. "I've just seen Mrs. Garrison, and she says that that gentleman is Mr Inspector Warder and he's of Scotland Yard – one of the tip-top men."

"Oh!" I rejoined. "Mrs. Garrison is indiscreet."

"But what's he doing here?" asked Mrs. Rooney. "I ain't got no thieves nor no burglars in the house."

"Of course you haven't," I said; "but you know poor Mr. Byrne has nearly been killed, and surely you don't want that matter to pass without being enquired into."

"Oh, is that it? You don't mean to say so. Of course you can't expect a poor widow with her old man dead these ten years—"

"Of course I can't," I said. "Don't you trouble your head about it, and don't tell anybody who that gentleman is, even now that you do know; especially not Mr. Byrne."

"Hush!" She put her finger to her lip in token of understanding and walked downstairs, as if thereby putting her seal upon the promise of secrecy.

On the Monday morning I was sitting in Byrne's room. He had got up and was turning out a number of odds and ends from his trunk. Sprat, who had become quite friendly with my neighbour, was prowling about the room, poking his little nose into this corner and into that, sniffing in all sorts of places. He had come across a little packet wrapped in brown paper, which was lying near the heap which Byrne had turned out of his box, and he commenced to sneeze violently, and tapped the thing with his paw, trying to turn it over.

"Oh, please leave that alone, Master Sprat," said Byrne jocularly. "It mightn't be good for you if you threw that about."

I picked the thing up. It was rather a heavy little parcel, about six inches long and three inches broad, and as deep. I felt it, and it gave a hard metallic resistance to my touch.

"What's this?" I asked.

"Oh," said Byrne, looking at me cautiously for a while, and then pulling himself together, "you're a good sort. You've been a true friend in need, and I don't mind telling you. That's one of my inventions. It's a Christmas toy – a surprise box. I wanted to take out a patent for it, and" – here he looked at me again, and paused for a moment – "that villain Brodie promised to lend me the money." This was the first mention of Brodie's name that had escaped his lips; but as I evinced no surprise he went on:

"You see," he said, opening the parcel and, to my astonished eyes, producing three little boxes identical with that diabolical one that had killed Lord Senfrey, "you send one of these to a friend. He opens it, and finds himself in the midst of a glare of red or green fire, and he thinks Satan has jumped out of the box in flames. It's harmless enough, though it might frighten timid people."

I felt the colour fade out of my cheeks, and I had to hold my breath.

"Do you make these things?" I gasped.

"Oh, yes, of course," he said. "I make lots of things like that. I'm always making things like that. Only, it's just my luck; I never can get anybody to work my inventions."

I looked at one of the little boxes; but he took it out of my hand.

"And how do you work it?" I asked, while my heart thumped against my ribs.

"You see this little band fastened to the bottom of the box by the tiny, securely soldered clip," he said, pointing out each particle as he went on. "That's the detonator. The slightest rupture will cause an explosion, which will set fire to the phospho-tinder next to it, and thus to the red, blue or green fire with which the box is filled. When you want to send it so that it can be opened without an explosion, you leave the detonator hanging loose inside, as it is now. But if you wish a show of fireworks, you carefully pull the detonator through this little aperture on the top of the box; you close the box in the same guarded manner: then you fasten the detonating band to the outside by this tiny clip, which you close upon it, cutting off if necessary the superfluous part of the band." He had suited his action to the words. "Now take the box in your hand, and open it," he added.

I did as I was told, and the result was a glare of red fire and red smoke, which filled the room. I quickly dropped the box on the little table by my side, for it was getting red hot.

All this while I felt as if a ball were sticking in my throat and were choking me.

"You say," I asked, "that Count Brodie promised to help you to patent this toy?" I had intentionally called Brodie "Count" so as to let him know that I knew the scoundrelly Maltese. He again looked at me enquiringly, but after a momentary pause simply answered, "Yes." He was evidently a shrewd man and a deep one. Was he trying to pump me by leading me on? I did not care.

"Did you give any of these things to Count Brodie?" I ventured to question.

The reply was prompt: "I sent three to him a little over a fortnight ago, when he was staying with Lord and Lady Bent at Farlowe Towers."

"A little over a fortnight ago?" I asked, hardly believing my ears.

"Yes," he said, "a little over a fortnight ago. I remember it well, because it was on my birthday, May the eleventh. But he swears that he never got them."

I rose and approached a little more closely.

"Do you know, Mr. Byrne," I asked, "that Lord Senfrey was murdered shortly after that through a box exactly similar to this one?"

"Of course I know that," he answered, without hesitation. "If it hadn't been for that, I should have tried to bring it out myself, but Brodie begged and prayed of me to let it rest for a while."

"But if the boxes didn't reach him, what had he to fear?" I demanded.

"I can't say," was the rejoinder. "He swears that he never got them. But, you see, he isn't the kind of man who would care to have his mode of life enquired into."

"Will you make me a present of a couple of these?" I said.

"By all means," he answered. "I don't know who you are," he added, looking straight at me, "nor why you've taken such an interest in me; and," he went on slowly and deliberately, "I'm not going to enquire, unless you tell me of your own accord. All I know is that but for you I should be a dead man at this hour. You saved my life, and this is but a little thing I can do for you. I was afraid to speak about this up to now, because one never knows how a man might be dragged into a business that he knows nothing about. Brodie said that the things never reached him; but he's such a liar, you know. People might have said that I had a hand in this dreadful murder, but I assure you that I had not, nor do I know how it was accomplished. My boxes may frighten people, but they wouldn't hurt them, nor could they kill a rat unless they were tampered with."

When I went back to my room after that, I sat down for a while in silent triumph. The proofs of the murderer's guilt were in my hands. Those diabolical boxes – the piece of paper, part of a sheet such as was constantly used in Lord Bent's house – the lettering upon it written with a "J" pen sideways – Lady Bent's habitual writing – and last of all, Lord Senfrey's letter to Brodie, which showed that the writer was aware of the Lady Bent's bigamous marriage, and thus gave a motive for the crime – all pointed unmistakably to Brodie and Lady Bent as accomplices in the dastardly deed.

I was just deliberating upon what would be the wisest course to take, when Mrs. Rooney ushered Luigi Orano into my room.

Chapter 11

A Life For a Life

ORANO bowed with the same formal and courtly grace which I had noticed on the previous occasion. "I come again," he said, with a forced smile; "I not able stay away."

He seated himself on the chair by the bedside, stroking the coverlet with his open palm. I saw that he made several fruitless attempts to speak, while his eyes wandered hither and thither all over the room, as if in search of the spirit that had fled out of that chamber to the great Unknown.

"I find t'e place," he went on, with a tremulous voice, "where t'ey bury her." He shook his head. "Shocking!" he said. "It break my heart."

I sat silently by for a while, deliberating with myself whether or not this could be the kind of man to trust with the knowledge that the scoundrel Brodie had destroyed his sister's happiness, and thereby her life. I reflected, however, that I intended to have the villain laid by the heels before the day was out; and, therefore, not much danger could arise.

"I'm glad you've come, Signor Orano," I said, "because I've something to communicate to you which will, at any rate, alter your opinion about the dead Lord Senfrey."

He leaned forward.

"Yes! Yes! Yes!" he exclaimed eagerly. "You have to say – What have you to say? Tell me. I am waiting. I am anxious."

"You'd better come with me into the next room. The man who lives there has resided in this house all the while your sister occupied this room. He will be able to give you much information."

He rose tremblingly. His eyes gleamed feverishly, and I saw that his teeth were hard set.

"Well! Well!" he cried, with feeble hoarseness. "I am waiting."

I led the way.

"Mr. Byrne," I said, when I had knocked and entered the other room, "this is Signor Luigi Orano."

Byrne looked up and gasped slightly; but he steadied himself.

"Oh yes," he answered, in a voice of perfect commonplace, "I know the gentleman. He is brother of the girl who killed herself in the next room."

"Yes," he interposed. "I am her brother. The gentleman," he went on, pointing to me, "he promise you can tell me somet'ing about her."

Byrne's looks wandered from Orano to me, and from me back to Orano.

"What do you want me to say?" he asked me, at last.

"I want you to tell this gentleman," I said, fixing my gaze upon Byrne, so that he flinched under it and had to cower back, "that it was not Lord Senfrey, but Gyffa Brodie, who enticed his sister to this place."

Byrne again looked at me shiftily, and paused for a moment or two in silence.

"Mr. Byrne," I said, "I expect you to tell the truth."

"Well," he retorted, with a slight shiver, "I think, perhaps, it is better that I should tell the truth, and have it off my chest. Brodie got this gentleman's sister to come and live here, so that he could call on her without his business being known. He used to come and see me, and from my room he could easily get into the next one without Mrs. Rooney being aware of it. How far his connection with the girl went, I don't know. He never stayed here more than an hour or so."

Orano had risen, with his face an olive grey, and a half insane glint in his eye. He babbled some incoherent words in Italian, and then looked at Byrne and at me.

"Say again," he gasped at last, pantingly. "I not believe I hear."

Byrne hesitated; but I was not to be baffled.

"Oblige the gentleman," I said. "Repeat what you said just now."

Byrne's face had gone nearly-white in the task. There was a terrible dread written upon every feature.

"I don't like this," he said; "and I see no advantage in it."

"Do it to oblige me," I said.

"Your sister," Byrne repeated slowly and hesitatingly, "came here at Count Brodie's instigation, and for the purpose of being able to be visited by him."

"Lord Senfrey never come here?" Orano hissed between his teeth, peering into Byrne's eyes as if he wished to scorch the truth out of them.

"Never," answered Byrne.

"That you swear?" was the fervent question.

"Lord Senfrey never came here. That I can swear," Byrne repeated.

Orano stood looking round the place like one dazed, Then he moistened his lips with his tongue, and after a gasp or two, put his hat on his head and walked out without saying a word.

"That man will kill Brodie," said Byrne, "if he can catch him; and a good riddance it will be of a filthy hound."

"I don't think he will kill Brodie," I retorted.

"And why not, pray?" asked Byrne.

"Because he'll not get the chance, I think. I shall have Brodie arrested today for attempting to poison you."

Byrne rose, and crossing his arms over his chest stood in front of me.

"Who are you, if I may ask?" he demanded.

"You know who I am," I replied.

"I know who you say you are," he went on determinedly, "and I know that you saved my life. That covers a lot of things. But you're not doing all this, and you've not done all this, simply because you love me so, for it doesn't stand to reason. What's your game?"

"You'll find that out soon enough," I went on; "and if you'll be reasonable, I'll take care that no harm comes to you."

"But if I'm not reasonable?" he rejoined sturdily, and, as I thought, viciously.

"Well," I said, "in that case, I should not be able to prevent certain disagreeable events which might or might not occur."

He walked up and down, and then looked at me again.

"You don't look like a detective," he said; "but I'd like to bet a sovereign to a penny piece that you are one, and a devilishly clever one."

"You've got your life," I said. "You yourself say that without me you would be a dead man. Be thankful for small mercies, and trust to Providence, or rather to me, for the rest."

A step on the landing, and the opening of my room door, attracted my attention at that moment, and going into my little apartment, I found Warder there.

"Well, G. G.," said the inspector effusively, "how are we getting on?"

"Like a house on fire," I replied. "I'm going to keep my promise to you today, and you shall collar one of the biggest villains of our day."

The inspector's eyes gleamed.

"Bravo!" he said. "That's a promise well kept. And who is the gentleman, pray?"

"The gentleman," I said, "is the man who calls himself Gyffa Brodie—"

"Count, if you please."

"Oh, I know the gentleman," replied the inspector, "and I've had my eye on him for a long time. I always thought there was something fly about him, only he kept such deuced good company."

"That man in the next room," I said, "is well enough today to go with you to Bow Street or wherever you like, and to apply for a warrant for that man's arrest on the charge of inciting those men in the Belvedere Road to murder him. You'd better go with him and take out a warrant and execute it, and I'd like to be with you when you do execute it."

"Right!" said the inspector. "You stroke my back, and I'll stroke your back. You shall come with me, and the little job shall be carried out in the most approved first-class style."

"Now," I said, "if you don't mind, we'll go and see Mr. Byrne."

My neighbour opened his eyes wide when I introduced the inspector to him.

"This," I said, "is Mr. Inspector Warder of the Criminal Investigation Department, and I've brought him to you for the purpose of seeing you righted. Up till now you were not strong enough to bear any excitement, but today you're well enough to apply for a warrant against that scoundrel Brodie for having attempted to murder you."

Byrne was sitting on the side of his bed as I spoke, and moved his legs uneasily.

"Brodie?" he said, as if endeavouring to gain time. "You want me to apply for a warrant against Brodie?"

"Yes," I replied; "I know that it was he who instigated those other people to murder you. If I hadn't been perfectly aware of that fact I should never have attempted to rescue you. Now you've got the whole truth of it."

"You want to get Brodie arrested on the charge of attempting to murder me?" Byrne asked, with a nearly vacant stare.

"Yes; and you'd better put your hat on and go with this gentleman to Bow Street," I said.

Byrne sat still.

"You don't seem to be very eager on this job, Mr. – Mr. Byrne, I believe," interposed Warder.

Byrne still sat hesitating.

"You see," he said, "there are wheels within wheels. I'm out of his clutches now, and I'll take care I don't get into them again; and, if I might be left alone, I'd prefer it."

Warder looked at me that moment. I slightly nodded my head, and the detective understood me perfectly.

"Mr. Byrne," he said, "I think I've got a little to say in this matter as well. You tell me that that man Brodie attempted to murder you, or incited other people to murder you. Now, whether you like it or whether you don't, murder and attempted murder are both offences that we cannot allow to go unpunished, and you'll just have to come."

"Oh!" retorted Byrne. "Have to?"

"You have not borne in mind my promise," I said. "I'll take care that as little inconvenience as possible shall befall you if you come with us."

He looked at me with a nervous enquiry.

"If not?" he asked.

"If not," I said, "I shall let matters take their course."

He sat for another moment or two swinging his legs to and fro. Then he jumped up.

"All right," he said, "if it has got to be, it has got to be, so here goes," and he put on his hat.

That very forenoon the warrant was granted, and whilst Byrne returned to James' Street, followed at a short distance by two trusty representatives of the detective police, Warder and myself went to the Olympian Club. It was about luncheon time, and I thought that very probably Brodie would be there at that time of day. The hall-keeper, however, informed us that Brodie had not yet been to the club that morning.

"He's sure to come here within the next half-hour," he said, "for I've three or four letters for him, and two of them are marked important."

"George," said a cheery voice at that moment, "what are you doing here?"

I looked round, and saw General Massinger.

"Business," I replied, with a smile, "partly of my own, partly of yours, General."

"Business of mine?" asked the old soldier with a quaint surprise.

"Yes, business of yours," I said. "It's about your friend, Count Gyffa Brodie."

"*My* friend?" snorted the General in disgust. "*My* friend? Hang the fellow! I'd hang him myself if they would let me have my way with him. He's a rogue – a clever rogue, but a dirty rogue."

"Quite right," I said. "It's for that reason I came. This gentleman here," I added, pointing to Warder, "is a police inspector, and he's going to rid your club of the Count for some time, at any rate."

The General stepped up to Warder and gripped him by the hand and shook it warmly.

"Thank you," he said, "thank you. If you don't mind," he added with gusto, "I'll stay and see it done."

"I don't mind in the least," rejoined the inspector; "the more the merrier."

It was agreed that Warder should wait under the portico, whilst I and the General watched from within the closed doors. Two of Warder's men were ready at the street corner to give assistance if necessary.

Fully half an hour elapsed before I saw Brodie sauntering leisurely up the street. He looked right and left, as if searching for hidden foes. At a short distance from the club he paused and gazed steadily in front of him, but no enemy being visible to his mind, he went on. The moment he passed into the portico, Warder put his hand upon his shoulder.

"I want to speak to you, sir," the officer said.

"To me?" replied Brodie, turning pale at the words.

"Yes, to you," said Warder. "I am Inspector Warder, of the Metropolitan Police, and I arrest you on the charge of complicity in an attempted murder."

Brodie staggered back, and leaned against the column of the portico, as if about to faint. He roused himself, however, and stretched out a fumbling hand towards his pocket. Warder was upon him in an instant and gripped him firmly, while the two men from the street corner came running up at top speed.

In the selfsame flash of time, however, a man rushed out from the semi-gloom of the next portico. Warder had pinioned Brodie from behind, and Luigi Orano, for it was he, sprang upon the Maltese, and holding a revolver point-blank in his face, fired.

The detective jumped back with a little cry, whilst a red shower splashed all over him and over the hall door window.

Brodie gave a wild jump into the air, and fell to the ground.

The two policemen, who had come to their inspector's assistance, made a dash at the Italian, but before they could secure him, two more shots stabbed the air, and two more bullets buried themselves in Brodie's body.

General Massinger and myself had swung open the hall door and rushed out in horror.

My precautions had been useless. The Italian had avenged his sister.

Chapter 12

Mystery, Thy Name is Man

A VILLAIN had been sent to his last account, and a wretched woman had been rid of a man who was dragging her with him on a career of crime. Even as I stood and looked down upon the gore-stained face of the murdered man, the thought flashed into my mind, "How will this affect Lady Bent?"

My plans had been carefully laid. With the Maltese behind lock and key on a charge totally different from the one I was instructed to investigate, my enquiries could be carried on with discretion, and without undue hurry. So much depended upon trifle, that I deemed sufficient indications to myself, but which were only proof in embryo, totally unfitted to be handed to a prosecuting counsel, that this sudden catastrophe seemed to me to scatter them all with a rude shock.

Luigi Orano had delivered his revolver to the man who arrested him without resistance, and he allowed himself to be led away like a child. There was a ghastly courtesy in his remark to Jerningham: "I am sorry, sir, if I have frightened you. I not could help it."

One clear result had sprung from Brodie's awful death – namely, the absolute proof of Lord Senfrey's guiltlessness of any illicit connection with Maria Orano. I could assure that broken-hearted girl, widowed without having been a wife, that the memory of her dear dead was untarnished. But what terror lay in store for that household if the honoured wife of that trusting, that upright, that noble-minded husband, were proven to be the accomplice of a murderer! I made up my mind at that moment to try my utmost to stay the blow. The real assassin, I thought, had met with his doom. He, at any rate, was the instigator, and that poor woman could not have been, to say the worst of it, more than a tool in his hands – a frightened, abjectly miserable, involuntary tool, I thought. Her whole life's history before she married this scoundrel, and after her marriage, pointed to such a conclusion.

The first thing to discover was whether or not Brodie actually received the parcel sent by Byrne. The villain had denied ever obtaining possession of it. But that was nothing. Such a man would lie with a smile upon his face at the slightest provocation – much more so when he thought his precious neck in danger.

Dear old General Massinger, who had watched Brodie's arrest with every mark of glee depicted on his weather bronzed face, looked grave when he quietly shook my hand as I was about to go away.

"I didn't want the rogue to be killed," the old soldier said. "I wanted him to be laid by the heels and kicked out; but this is much more terrible than I ever expected. He must have been mixed up in a lot of villainy."

"He has, dear General," I replied – "more than you can guess at present."

"At this the old soldier's spirits seemed to revive. I thought so," he said. "I never liked his looks, George; and I said to Colonel Vicar only yesterday, 'Vicar,' I said, 'that man will be hanged!' and, to tell you the truth, I'm rather sorry I was wrong."

I walked away from the Olympian Club with a load upon my mind. I was honour bound to bring the news of the dreadful event immediately to Rhowdon House. At that time I was not schooled in the necessities and exigencies of my profession as I became soon after, and I rather dreaded the task. I quickly saw, however, that procrastination would be worse than useless, and therefore took a cab to Park Lane.

"The Earl's with my Lady and Lord and Lady Senfrey in the study," said the portly old hall-keeper, in reply to my query if Lord Bent were in the house; and I felt that I had arrived in the midst of a small family conclave; and, as a matter of fact, when I was ushered into the rather sombre and old-fashioned apartment, I found myself with quite a little crowd of people. Lady Bent and Lady Senfrey were sitting on a big Chesterfield sofa, and Lady Georgina was leaning back languidly in an armchair by her stepmother's side. Lord Senfrey was nervously fidgeting on a stiff-backed old oak chair at the head of the writing-table, whilst opposite the Earl, and facing me, in the centre of the writing-table, sat Mr. Oscar Plume, evidently busily engaged with something or other, for I could hear his pen travelling over the paper.

The Earl rose as I entered, and came to me and held out his hand.

"I'm glad to see you, George," he said; "you come just at the right moment. We were wondering if we were nearer any probable solution of the terrible mystery."

I looked round, and my eyes met those of Lady Bent. She flushed beneath my gaze, and I saw her turn pale. A pitiful glance, like a prayer for mercy, shot from her eyes towards me, and callous as I thought I was, I felt it quiver through me. How would she bear the news I brought?

But another pair of eyes caught mine at that moment – languid, beseeching, trustful – Lady Georgina's. There was a prayer of hope in that look, a hope begotten of the love that was buried and yet alive – of the love that had never been allowed to ripen, and that yet was bearing bitter fruit. That glance nerved me to my task, for here I had an unquestionable and unquestioned duty to perform.

"I've come, Lord Bent," I said, "as the bearer of grave news." Lady Bent sat upright at this moment, and I saw that she clutched the upholstery of the sofa nervously, as she had gripped the pillow on the day I had last seen her. "I am the bearer of terrible news, even though they bring comfort in their way."

"Now, don't go and frighten us, Mr. Grey," chimed in Lady Senfrey. "If there's anything awful or shocking I don't want to hear it. I've had enough of the whole business. Poor Alfred is dead, and there's an end to it. I'm nervous this morning, and not at all well."

Lady Bent had caught Lady Senfrey's hand, and, without looking at her, said: "Have patience, my dear. It's our duty to listen."

"I am sure," I said, "I don't wish to distress Lady Senfrey, and if she's likely to be shocked by what I have to tell, I would prefer she were not here."

Lady Bent's face had gone white, but I could see her set her teeth hard in a despairing effort to appear calm.

"You really must hear what Mr. Grey has to say, Agatha," interposed Lord Senfrey. "It may be disagreeable, but it is a duty. Let us bear it as a duty."

There was a pause of a moment, during which the movement of Mr. Oscar Hume's pen ever travelling over the paper produced the only sound audible in the room.

"I suppose I am at liberty to speak?" I said, and the Earl slightly nodded his head.

"Go on, George," he said.

I advanced two or three steps towards Lady Georgina and addressed her.

"Lady Georgina," I said, "you have specially charged me to prove that Lord Senfrey was guiltless of any illicit connection with that girl, Orano. I am happy to say that that fact was absolutely proven this morning."

I could see Lady Bent heave a sigh of relief. Her stepdaughter rose and advanced towards me.

"Speak, Mr. Grey," she said. "Speak; I am listening."

"Your intended husband was absolutely sinless in this matter," I said. "The seducer of that girl has been discovered, and he was killed not half an hour ago by the girl's brother, who had found out his treachery to his sister."

The poor girl did not know whether or not to thank me but she smiled painfully, and retreating as slowly as she had advanced, sank down into her chair again.

"Thank God!" she said. "My Alfred's memory is saved. Thank God for that!"

There was another pause. Then Lord Bent asked: "And who is the man who was killed?"

"Count Brodie," I replied.

Lady Bent rose with her eyes wide open and her arms abroad. Her lips were apart, as if she were choking. She gasped for a second or two, and then her eyes closed, and she would have fallen headlong to the floor had I not jumped forward and caught her, and placed her gently back on the sofa.

Lady Senfrey and Lady Georgina had risen. Lord Senfrey had rushed to Lady Bent, and the only person who seemed to be totally unmoved by the announcement was Mr. Hume, who had stayed his pen and was looking on without a sign. He rose quietly at last, and said, "Shall I call my Lady's maid, my Lord?"

"You'd better ring for her, I think," said Lord Bent, who had gone to his wife and was fanning her with his handkerchief. "The momentary excitement of this terrible news has shocked and prostrated her. The surprise must have been awful. It nearly took my breath away."

The maid came with other women, and Lady Bent reluctantly followed her. As she passed me, she shot a glance towards me which, whether it were one of prayer or one of thanks, I could not tell. It was some time before equanimity of mind was restored in that little conclave, and then Lord Bent asked me to be seated.

"All this, though very awful, is very comforting for my poor child," said the old man, "for the villain seems to have met his deserts. There's little doubt in my own mind that poor Senfrey was murdered because he was wrongly suspected of this treachery. Have you advanced any further in your enquiry about this?"

"That's another point about which I've come," I said, "and with which the name of Brodie is inextricably intermingled. May I ask you, Lord Bent, if you remember Brodie staying with you at Farlowe, a little over a fortnight ago?"

"Of course I remember that," said Lord Bent.

"Will you please tell me," I went on, "who during your stay at Farlowe is the person charged with receiving the parcels and letters which arrive there?"

Mr. Hume, who had resumed his writing, stopped at this question and looked at me.

"Mr. Hume will explain that better than I can," said the Earl. "Will you please tell Mr. Grey, Mr. Hume?"

The sphinx-like face was hard drawn. The cold grey eyes were looking straight at me, and then flashed across to Lady Georgina and back to me again, as if a sudden emotion had passed through the man's mind and vanished.

"All letters and parcels," he said, "for my Lord and my Lady or for Lady Georgina are taken straight to their rooms by their servants. All letters or parcels for any of the guests are brought to me, and I send them to the different rooms or deliver them myself, or have them delivered, wherever the ladies and gentlemen may be."

"Do you remember, Mr. Hume," I asked, "whether on May the eleventh or twelfth last a small parcel arrived at Farlowe addressed to Count Brodie?"

The impenetrable face quivered with a slight start. The lips closed tightly. There was a moment's pause as of reflection.

"I think I remember such a parcel," Hume said, at last.

"Can you tell," I continued, "whether that parcel was delivered into Count Brodie's hands?"

"What a question!" interposed the Earl. "Of course it would have been delivered to him."

"I must repeat my question," I said determinedly, "because the Count has stated that that parcel never reached him, and I would ask Mr. Hume to rack his memory so as to be able to tell us for certain whether or not on May the eleventh or twelfth Count Brodie received a little parcel about six inches long and three inches broad and deep, and when and where that parcel was delivered to him."

The secretary rose slowly. Again there was that swift impassioned glance towards Lady Georgina, followed by the same impenetrable coldness.

"I shall have to go upstairs," he said quietly, "because I have a little book there which will enable me to give the precise information."

With that he slowly walked out of the room, looking neither to the right nor to the left.

The servants had returned in the meantime and told us that Lady Bent had recovered, and had sent word that she would be down again nearly immediately. My place was a very awkward one, as, try how I might, I had to turn my back upon some of the people present. I therefore stepped behind the table and sat myself down on the secretary's chair and waited. As I did so, my glance fell quite casually on the writing in front of me. It was a document written in French in a bastard French legal round hand, in which all the small letters were exquisitely and perfectly formed, but all the capitals were simply printed Roman letters imitated in writing.

The writing attracted me, and especially the word "*Résumé*" which headed it. I thought I had seen that "R" before, and in the selfsame instant I recognised it. The thought was so surprising that it nearly made me shiver. In my pocket there was that slip torn from the paper which had enveloped the poisoned box. I fumbled in my waistcoat, and pulled it out and stole a glance towards it. It was absolutely the same "R."

It was written in the same way with the pen held sideways, and as I looked on the paper in front of me, it was the self-same kind of paper, taken from a De la Rue eighteenpenny packet.

I had barely time to grasp the whole extent of my discovery, and its possible effect, when screams were heard, and one of the servants came rushing into the room.

"My lords, my ladies, there's something going on! There's a terrible smoke coming out of Mr. Hume's room, and nobody can get near it."

We all started to our feet. I do not remember how the others received the news, but I flew helter-skelter upstairs in the direction pointed out by the scared and white-faced servants, who were lining the staircase.

There was no difficulty in finding the place. On the second floor already a dense and acrid vapour gripped the throat and nostrils with a poisonous clutch. I tried to dash into it, but a single gasp proved to me that it was deadly. Luckily I had time to dart back out of it ere it could get full hold upon me. Even then, my head swam, my eyes appeared to be on fire, the blood had started to my throat, and I felt as if it were about to pour from my eyes, nose and lips.

I jumped back to the landing, and stood there helpless: Two or three of the men-servants were there looking at one another in horrified amazement, whilst the women were grouped lower down wringing their hands.

As I looked around, I saw Lord Bent at my side. The old nobleman's face had gone nearly as white as his hair.

"Terrible!" he said, "terrible! The hand that murdered Lord Senfrey is in this." Then he turned with a serenity of quiet self-possession to his servants. "Open every window on this floor," he said. "You, Robinson, go with any two of the others by the servants' staircase to the fourth floor. Take a fire escape into the room over Mr. Hume's and lower yourself out of the window on to the little balcony outside Mr. Hume's room. Tie a handkerchief over your mouth and nose. Take a hatchet with you, and try to open Mr. Hume's door, and if you fail, break the window. But, whatever you do, keep the fire escape rope round you, and the moment you've opened or broken the window, let the others pull you up with all possible speed."

After that we waited for nearly ten minutes. Then a servant brought news that the man sent to do the work had broken Mr. Hume's window and had been pulled up from the balcony by his comrades in the nick of time and nearly unconscious.

Another terrible quarter of an hour passed before the currents of fresh air which were everywhere established rendered access to the next floor possible. Then one by one we crept up. I had asked for a small wet sponge, which I placed into my mouth and tied a handkerchief over it and over my nostrils. Even then I staggered and reeled like a drunken man as I reached the door.

"Break it open!" said Lord Bent quietly from below, "if it's locked."

One of the men had brought a fireman's axe, and with a crash the panels flew into splinters.

Again we had to retreat, for the poisonous fumes that came towards us were still nearly deadly. A few more smashes against the woodwork, and the door lay in pieces.

Yet another interval elapsed before we dared to venture into the place, Hume was seated at his table. His arms were stretched out in front of him, and his head had fallen upon them; and just in front of him a little tin box stood open.

It was another of those diabolical engines.

I raised his head. It was heavy as lead, and, escaping from my grasp, fell back upon his hands. I took one of the hands. They were icily cold.

The man was dead.

As I glanced around, I saw a sheet of notepaper upon the table, and on it I read these lines:

LADY GEORGINA—

I loved you with the love of despair. Since you were a child, I held you, my goddess, unapproachable, sacred. That a mortal like myself should possess what I worshipped I deemed sacrilege. Fate placed a weapon in my hand, and I destroyed him who dared to claim you as his own. As a fitting sequel of sacrifice, I now offer my life. My last breath is perfumed by a vow of love that will endure beyond the grave. Forgive a man who loved not wisely but too well. I dare not say forget.

OSCAR HUME.

The medical minds were sorely exercised in this case, as in Lord Senfrey's, about the poison used. But at last they discovered that it was a venom brought by Hume from Africa. It was found to be the powdered extract of a poisonous seed, much resembling the Tanghinia Venenifera, or Madagascar poison, and, like that seed, used by the natives as an ordeal and arrow poison, only much swifter and more terrible in its effects. A small quantity of the powder, of an iron-grey colour, was found at the bottom of a little box in which Hume had kept it; and its analysis led to the proof.

A week after the terrible events just recorded I was again in Lord Bent's study. His wife and daughter were with him.

"I suppose it's unnecessary now to keep this envelope which you confided to me a little while ago?" Lord Bent asked.

"Open it, pray open it, my lord," I rejoined.

A moment afterwards he held the ten-pound note and the little scrap of paper in his hand.

"Did he think he could buy my soul for ten pounds?" he read; and added, "What does this mean?"

"It is the proof of the late Lord Senfrey's absolute guiltlessness," I replied. "I had gone to live in the room where that Italian girl killed herself. One night I was kept awake by my little dog – the late Lord Senfrey's little dog – Sprat, whining and growling at something; and I rose to discover what it all meant. I could see nothing, but Sprat jumped on to the windowsill, where two flowerpots stood, and in his excitement he knocked down one of them. When I picked up the pieces I found, hidden beneath the mould, this note and this scrap of paper – 'Did he think he could buy my soul for ten pounds,' – and this ten-pound note."

"Did that poor girl write these words?" asked Lord Bent quietly.

I replied, "Undoubtedly; and if you will have this note traced, you will find that it was issued by your bankers to yourself."

"To me?" asked Lord Bent, in amazement. "To me?"

"Yes," I answered, "to your lordship. It was given," I said, keeping a fixed gaze on Lady Bent, "by you to her ladyship, and by her ladyship, in settlement of some trifling account, to Brodie."

A look of gratitude gleamed in the poor woman's eyes which went straight to my heart.

"It is well," said Lord Bent. "It shall be applied, with others, for her brother's defence."

Lady Georgina had stepped to my side, and looked into my eyes, "You say, Mr, Grey," she whispered, "that my Alfred's little dog found these things. It is Sprat, of course. I had forgotten all about him. Have you got him now?"

"Yes," I answered, "of course I have."

"Will you give him to me?" she pleaded. "Do please, Mr. Grey, grant me this favour. Give him to me."

I felt a momentary twinge. I was loath to part with my little doggie, but I knew that in that girl he would find a kind and more than patient mistress; and, after all, she had more right to him than I.

"You shall have him, Lady Georgina," I said. "I will bring him to you today."

I do not know to this day whether I was right or wrong. The moralist may say "Nay," but many people will agree with me in thinking that, after all, it was wiser and more just that I should preserve the honour and happiness of that already sorely stricken household. I kept the story of Lady Bent's previous career from the world. I made arrangements for the poor woman with Byrne, by which, in consideration of a sum of money paid to him, he agreed to leave England and for ever to keep silence. I personally place little faith in the promise of that kind of man, but Lady Bent felt a weight off her heart when she knew that Jasper Byrne had gone to America.

"To think of you being a detective, Mr. Grant," cried Mrs. Rooney, when I again stood in the little room in James' Street. "You of all the people in this world! I always did think that policemen in plain clothes was awkward, gawky chaps with big boots and big sticks, and you looking so nice, and being so gentlemanly! Well, wonders will never cease. I'm sorry, I am, that you're going away, for it isn't often that a poor widow with seven children to keep, and one of them a cripple from 'is birth, and her old man dead and gone these ten years—"

"Yes, Mrs. Rooney," I replied, "it isn't. But I'm coming back to you now and then, and you haven't seen what I've brought with me."

I pointed to a small hamper.

Mrs. Rooney crept towards it as if it were something alive. She untied the string and opened it.

"Why," she exclaimed, "it is – it isn't – yes, of course it is – it's gin, and all these bottles – are they for me?"

"It's a present of a dozen for you – of a round dozen – to keep you warm when the nights get colder."

Mrs. Rooney looked at me for a moment. Then she held out her arms.

"You're a duck!" she cried, "and I *must* kiss you."

I bore the infliction like a martyr, and smiled.

THE END

Visit Oleander to view all
titles and sign up to our
Newsletter

Death of an Editor
Vernon Loder

Murder on May Morning
Max Dalman

The Hymn Tune Mystery
George A. Birmingham

The Middle of Things
JS Fletcher

The Essex Murders
Vernon Loder

The Boat Race Murder
R. E. Swartwout

Who Killed Alfred Snowe?
J. S. Fletcher

Murder at the College
Victor L. Whitechurch

*The Yorkshire
Moorland Mystery*
J. S. Fletcher

Fatality in Fleet Street
Christopher St. John Sprigg

The Doctor of Pimlico
William Le Queux

The Charing Cross Mystery
J. S. Fletcher

<u>Free Golden Age Mystery</u>

Fatality in Fleet Street ePub
& PDF **FREE** when you sign
up for our infrequent
Newsletter.

Made in the USA
Monee, IL
12 November 2022

17586544R00094